Herakles

≈

A Fable

Bruce McLaren

Herakles - A Fable©
Bruce McLaren 2011
ISBN#9780615557298

To My Great Friend F

Contents

Spring

Summer

Autumn

Winter

Spring

CHAPTER ONE

The Old Man and the Sun

The old man stretched out his arms and studied the backs of his hands, tanned and creased, as old hands get.

His fingernails were lined.

He remembered how, as a boy, he would gaze in wonder at his father's serrated fingernails and compare them to his own child's nails, unblemished and polished like small sea shells, smoothed by the rolling surf.

Now he had his father's fingernails.

The old man considered his age.

Then he noticed the sunlight glinting off the small golden hairs, not yet grey, but still gold, on his forearms and the backs of his hands. The sun was speaking to him.

"There is life in you yet!" said the sun.

In gratitude, the old man drank in the warm rays.

He closed his eyes. The old man focused on the red, fiery world behind his eyelids, just as he had done when he was a young boy.

Surely, some things never change. Surely, he was now old, but he would always remain a boy.

"Ah sun my great friend. Greetings!"

"Greetings to you old man," replied the sun. "But you are not as old as you suppose. I am much older than you. But see how brightly I burn!"

"I admit, most wondrous orb, that for a moment I was thrown into melancholy. I have circled you many times on this earth and my span here is nigh. But I caught myself as I stumbled, for I will always be young, and in youth I shall pass on."

"An admirable approach! You are unlike other men, who shrivel in spirit with age. Be like me! For I too shall pass on. But I shall not fizzle out like a damp fuse. Oh no! I shall collapse in upon myself and explode in great glory."

"Your words give me happiness," said the old man. "They are fitting for one of your state, a sublime sphere coursing with power and unbridled intensity. Your destiny is glory. Your attribute is pride. Anything less than a love of yourself would be an insult, an insult to yourself! Truly you are great!"

"Hah!" said the sun. "Truly you speak truly!"

"But tell me, great sun, as you charge through the celestial realms in your fiery chariot, what do you see of man? For you have seen all, from the beginning, and will see all, to the end."

"Ah man," sighed the sun. "So much promise, but such unspeakable disgrace. Man strains for greatness yet remains incapable of attaining that goal. Man is possessed of genius but remains a hopeless fool. Truly a descendent of an ape! Gone are the days of the Aton and Mithras, and the times before, when all men saw fit to worship me."

"Oh life-giving sun, your dominion is so vast and your eye has seen so far. I ask you this, is there not one great man to grace this earth, to do honor to your most beautiful, blue daughter?"

"There is but one great man worthy of my daughter," said the sun. "There is but one great man to whom I would happily present a dowry. In fact, that man has already lain with her and has loved her and I have consented and loved him in return."

"Who is this man? Tell me, great sun, who could this most blessed man be?"

"You!" said the sun.

"Ah!" smiled the old man.

And the sun's rays kissed his lips.

CHAPTER TWO

The Old Man Converses With a Bee

The old man had been drifting, asleep. The shadows were long and the late afternoon light was transforming the complexion of the sky. Cerulean blues and deep violets spanned the horizon, furnished by rolling clouds, majestic in their gold and amber robes, deep purple shadows in their folds.

Spring.

The old man could sense it coming. The first wafts of tulips and hyacinth. He closed his eyes and breathed the perfume.

"Ah, I smell you my friends," said the old man. "You try to sneak up on me but you forget that I am still young. I have the nose of a child. And here you are once more, my playful auguries and messengers. Tell me, what does this season portend? Hah! And now I smell your laughter. You detect my joke. We both know there is only one portent, and that is good. There is only life, and what is life if not good? Let your herald sound and bring forth your friends in full bloom. Don't be shy. For it is spring! It is a time for birth. Let your friends surge forth in an unrestrained and boisterous wave. Wash forth!"

"To whom do you speak old man?"

The old man hesitated.

"From whence comes this voice? Do you not introduce yourself before you speak? Have you no manners? Who reared you so poorly?"

"I am a bee and I was reared by the queen."

"Aha. That explains it. The queen rears so many she has no time to teach. Well then, young bee, sit on my shoulder if you wish to converse."

"Thank you," said the bee, landing gently.

"So, to whom were you speaking, old man?"

"I was speaking to the flowers, to the tulips and the hyacinths."

"Why would you speak to flowers? Do you expect them to speak back?"

"Little bee, I converse with many things."

"But flowers don't speak! Old man, perhaps your mind has abandoned you? Perhaps you are losing your marbles? Perhaps, old man, you should be eating the flowers? Eating the flowers like crazy old men do."

"Do you know who else eats flowers, little bee?"

"Who?"

"Children. Children eat flowers. I remain a child, hence my greatness."

"You are great?" queried the bee, in mock amazement.

"Ah, sarcastic little bee. You jibe, but the truth is this. I am the greatest of men."

"According to whom?"

"The sun."

"Oh," said the bee, lowering its tone. "I apologize. I am young and rash. I am slow to think and quick to act."

There was a brief silence as the bee pondered.

"So old man, can you *really* talk to flowers?"

"Indeed. And also the sun. I can even talk to bees."

"Do you talk to other men?"

"No."

"Why?"

"I like to have intelligent conversations."

"Ah," said the bee. "That's why you seem like a crazy old man."

"When in fact I am the greatest man."

"Well then," said the bee, buzzing up into the air and hovering before the man's nose. "It has been a pleasure to meet you."

"No my little friend, it has been a pleasure for me to meet you, but it has been an honor for you to meet me."

"Oho!" laughed the bee as it hummed off in search of nectar. "Then you *are* the greatest man!"

The old man smiled and went back to sleep.

CHAPTER THREE

The Old Man Meets the Wasp

The grass was growing long about the old man's feet. A menagerie of insects careened through the foliage, darting about the violets and orchids, colliding in their haste, drunk with nectar.

Churning, pregnant clouds passed overhead, casting shadows across the lawn, offering respite from the now impulsive and capricious sun.

The old man's chair had been placed at the base of an old oak tree for shade, and he looked calmly out from beneath the brim of his hat.

A voice, rich in devilry sang into his ear, "Old man, what say I bite you?"

The old man had not felt the wasp land on his left shoulder.

"It is no coincidence you want to bite me on my left side you rogue. I sense the black arts in you."

"Nonsense. No-one believes in hobgoblins anymore. But you will believe in me when I drive my barb into your weak flesh! For I am the wasp and your thin skin would collapse under the weight of my sting."

The old man laughed.

"When I was young my skin was like leather and my hands moved like lightning. I would have crushed you already! But in my age I have grown great, and my greatness is measured by my wisdom. And my wisdom speaks thus,

"If you bite me I will still love you, but I'd rather you didn't bite me just the same."

"Impertinent old fool," said the wasp. "You don't get off that easily. I have heard talk about you. I have heard words borne on the wind. These words say you don't speak to other men. They say you are arrogant and vain. They say you have something of the wasp in you. Would you care for some more?"

"Dear wasp, you hear but lies born from misunderstanding. Some envy me my greatness. Some hate me because I fly so high. They look down as I approach. I sense their unease. They are ashamed. But I love them just the same, and I love their misunderstanding and incomprehension, and I even love their lies, for what are lies more than untruths?"

"You play with words old man. I sense something of the charlatan in you, and I intend to do you ill. You'll have to do better than that.

"You claim to love men and even their lies. So speak of love, oh wise and greatest lover! Let loose your tongue or I will let loose my sting!"

CHAPTER FOUR

The First Story

A vast plume of dust is kicked up by the car as it hurtles along the dirt road.

F is transfixed by the sight. He never tires of looking at it. The dust is powder-dry and buffets alongside the car. The car can never escape the cloud. And if they slow for a bend in the road then the cloud sweeps over them and passes on ahead, settling on their tongues and in their eyes, temporarily blinding them.

To F, this sensation is strangely akin to being subsumed in the disgorging exhalation of some primordial beast, some ancient phantasm that lurks in the belly of the land.

But they drive on nonetheless, trusting themselves to their knowledge of the road.

For this is their land.

The dust mingles with the thick, omnipresent fragrance of eucalyptus, the defining smell of 'the bush', the uncompromising and seemingly limitless domain of gum and iron-bark that clings to cliffs of sandstone or climbs out of shadowed ravines.

This land, the last to be settled by the white man, never designed by the hand of the creator to accommodate the white man, burnt and toughened, lethal and unforgiving, home to strange animals not found in other, softer climes. This land of isolation, of heat and fire and flood, brutal and untamed, through whose undergrowth crawls poison and danger.

This land, the Australian bush.

It is Sunday. Summer. And the fiery furnace of Vulcan is being funneled down the length of the valley.

They are driving home from church, father pushing the car as fast as it will go, for he too can hardly get away fast enough from the stifling sermons and stiff-necked parishioners.

Christmas. The one day of the year that mother enforces, nay, verily ordains, that the family *has* to go to church.

For this pilgrimage proves to the other parishioners that although they live way up in the top end of the valley they are not yet heathens engulfed by the wild, to demonstrate that they too have the necessary standards of the people of the town.

"*But why?*" thinks F.

Father, his duty done, is hurtling back into his own realm, to that of the top end of the valley, to the crops that he toils over and wars the land for in endless campaign. These battles are the rhythms that father is attuned to, being from the land. And the people of the town have no conception of, no awareness of, no appreciation of, and no unspoken love for, such things.

Father drives as if in a fever. F feels it too. Part relief, part homecoming, part the longing for the land, for the sensation of the bare-feet in the soil, for the sound of the tractor being started in the shed.

But don't forget there is also the sheer thrill of driving fast, recklessly, as fast as a horse going pell-mell, full-pelt across an open field.

There is the thrill of movement.

Then, finally, F is alone in the front paddock, hoe in hand, chipping weeds in the melon patch, with the easy contentment of the regular swing, the wooden handle worn smooth through use.

The roasting sun falls evenly on F's shoulders. His collar is up, His arms and legs are deeply tanned and his feet treading deftly and instinctively between the vines. The flash of the blade, with the sheen of a polished knife, never misses its target.

And as if coming out of a trance, F notices the first birds of the evening, the kookaburras calling down at the river, crying out,

"The sun is low. The shadows are crossing the valley!"

And F looks up to see the vivid colors of white cockatoos with sulfur crests, the purple and pink galahs, the soaring king parrots of royal reds and greens, flashing in brilliance against the seamless sky.

From the house up on the mountainside F can hear the distant sounds of pots and pans and dinner being prepared.

The house was built in the old times, by the settlers who knew how high the river would rise in flood.

Then, as twilight ebbs into darkness, F drops the hoe, where it will lie until he picks it up the following morning, and he walks up to the light on the hill.

Home.

The life of F is consumed with the land and, above all, the impenetrable and mysterious horizon of the bush.

Impenetrable, that is, to all but him.

Once, long ago, the aborigines had also moved through the bush, and they had known it far better than him.

But now they were gone.

The aborigines left their paintings in the sacred areas, the rudimentary pictures of kangaroos and the outlines of hands, the pigment of chewed and spat clay, the hands decrying,

"This is me. I was here. I am here!"

F knew where the paintings were. The old farmers in the top end of the valley also knew, for they too had once been boys themselves, and had also roamed far and wide. But they had aged and roamed no more.

F could navigate deep into the bush. He knew each gully and the aspect of each slope. He knew the best way up each mountain and he knew what lay beyond each ridge. He knew which ravines to avoid for brown-snakes and where to find kangaroo tracks. He would carefully study the droppings of the wallabies and picture in his mind when they had been there and wonder if they were still watching him, hidden, infinitely more attuned to the bush than he.

But F did know when and where the wallabies would appear to graze. He would climb a cliff in the late afternoon so he could spy them from above. Then he would hear the 'thump, thump, thump' leading right up to the small opening of bush grass. And F would gaze down at them in wonder.

One time F had even seen a wallaroo, that bastard half-breed of the kangaroo and the wallaby, powerful and thickset, aggressive and black, with claws that could gut you and a tail that could break your back. F had been following the wallaby trails, no more than a sliver through the bush, skipping from stone to stone to avoid any leaf-laying adders. His ears were young and sharp and detected the first distant pounding from a long way off. F darted into the scrub upslope and crouched down and hid and waited. The pounding grew louder, threatening and menacing, until F could see it approach, ominous and dark. And then at the point where F had left the trail the wallaroo stopped on an open rock and F could see it clearly. He held his breath.

Then in a mighty bound the wallaroo was off and across the gully and out of sight.

F knows all of these things and he knows them beneath both sun and moon.

F lives and breathes the land. And he is acutely aware that the land *also* breathes.

F knows that some of the old sacred aboriginal places are to be avoided. F can *feel* the oppressive and overbearing weight when he passes by, and he knows that ancient rites had been performed in those places and that the old spirits of the land still remain there even though the aborigines themselves had long moved on.

The old spirits of the land. The old nature spirits as old as the land itself. From the Gondwana times. Spirits beyond age. Shapeless and fearful.

How distant is F's world from that of other men. How absurd the farmers seem when viewed from high up on the mountains. They appear as mere gnats, gnawing and toiling away. F looks down at the houses and sheds.

Settlement. Sedentism.

F holds a deep aversion to such things. These inventions of man, these shackles imposed upon man by man himself. To F it is all beyond the absurd! What is this shed? What is this house? What is this church? What is this school?

Why are these things?

School, for F, means rising in the dark for bread and butter and then a ten mile walk.

The valley is more open here, the land less wild, the farms more numerous. And inside the school are thirty desks and chairs, for that is the total number of children in the valley, all classes combined, from seven years old to seventeen, everyone together.

Separating the young faces from the blackboard is the figure of Miss Brackenridge, peering at her students from behind her spectacles, with a wry smile, possessing knowledge she will rarely have cause to use with those allotted to her, capable of quoting Greek or Latin verse, secretly delighting in Virgil and Horace, musical, mathematical, poetic, yet somehow transported to this place so inappropriate to her. But she accepts it as her destiny nonetheless.

And behind her is the framed picture of the monarch in all her regalia, flanked by the Union Jack and the Australian flag, mother and child of empire.

"*What* is this place?" F thinks to himself.

Then he sees her. How his heart leaps like a stag!

Try as he might he can hardly stop his stare. With every turned page there is a sidelong glance.

His neck draws tight and he shivers.

"*Miranda.*"

Her name sounds translucent.

F has never seen anything so beautiful. With golden hair and steady blue eyes, she holds herself upright and noble. She flows in proportion, the line of her back curving down long like a waterfall. Her skin is the color of honey.

"*Miranda. Oh Goddess!*"

She turns and sees F looking at her. Her eyes flash and she smiles. Her face resonates with life.

His chest heaves and his pulse races. How could God have created such a thing?

And the creator spoke,

"*Witness boy the most beautiful product of my creative genius. Behold woman!*

"*You will love her and will fall over yourself just to glimpse her and she will enchant you with magic far beyond your understanding. And her smile will lift you up to the summits but will also drive you to madness and cast you down to the bottomless depths.*

"Behold boy, my creation!"

And from that moment on F's life is utterly transformed. For now, Miranda is constantly in his thoughts. When he sleeps she enters his dreams. And when he wakes she is instantly at the forefront of his mind.

F burns with an intensity. He aches.

The days pass in tortuous and excruciating charades of youth. The parades and performances as the boys eye the girls and the girls eye the boys and they each wonder what mysteries the other holds. F feels as if caught in a heavy undertow, dragging him down, relentlessly. His head swims.

Until finally, mercifully, the fateful day arrives, and F faces Miranda behind the schoolhouse and she stands there and studies him intently.

And for F that is the moment when everything changes. It is the pinnacle of moments.

What mystery!

That night F steals away and cuts through the bush by moonlight. His limbs are on fire, every muscle taut and strong, and his frame lean and stripped.

And now to be added to his life the heavy fuel of love! Can you see how he floats?

F soars across the terrain from on high, mercurial, raised up in approval by the land itself, passing evenly and knowingly over every gully and crest and gorge. For the great spirits are at work, irresistible spirits! The spirits of life, indomitable in action.

And F is more akin to a God than a man.

F can see her shadow against the school steps.

There she is, right before him. Her hair glistens as silver beneath the moon. They face one another and bring their foreheads together, silently, drawing close, and slowly drop to the steps, clasping each other tight.

And F wants to weep for happiness. For if there is never another moment, then this moment is enough.

F gently presses his lips against her eyelids and eyebrows, kissing her with a tenderness that woman is unsuspecting of in man. He touches her cheeks and ears and neck with his fingertips. F softly places his lips on hers, as if she is an idol of gold, something to be worshipped, something consecrated, something worthy of sacred adoration.

And there they remain, as if partaking as of a holy rite, until the first faint light of dawn unfolds in the distance. F kisses her again and again, and she laughs.

Then she is gone.

F now moves in a deranged fever. Nothing gives him solace. He burns to run through the bush, willing to tear himself to shreds on the red-hot wrought-iron gates of hell, just to see her.

But he doesn't have to wait long.

For there she is walking up to his house, her white dress glowing, her honeyed legs and bare-feet in the holy dirt.

She approaches F beneath the moon.

They walk at night in the bush and F shows her the rainforest in the gully that only he goes to, with giant hanging vines and lyre-birds, and they sit on cool mossy rocks, she on his lap, he kissing her neck and her lips, holding each other and listening to the water trickle out from the spring below.

And F marvels in delight at her skin so smooth and brown, and feels her legs that cross his own, lithe and tanned. And F is overwhelmed.

He takes her down to the poplar grove, the silver trunks posted like sentinels in rows, forming an ethereal and wondrous cathedral around them. They stand together in the moonlight and it is as if a wedding is taking place, a divine wedding, with the poplars as a guard of honor looking on in full approval.

F tells her that he loves her.

Then F takes her to the sacred places, with the timeless paintings, in the ominous and yawning caves of sandstone. And in the cave F builds a fire and they lie together and the wild shadows of the old spirits dance upon the sandstone, red and gold.

But then, an ill omen.

At school she stands aloof and is restrained. F's chest is torn apart.

"Oh creator! What torments to be found in your invention?"

He instinctively knows the reason. Her mother doesn't want Miranda to see F anymore. Her mother is moving her to the school in town. To get her away from him.

Miranda says she is sorry. What they had done was wrong. It had to stop.

F reels.

Now F cannot sleep. He wanders through the bush restlessly and aimlessly, with a new, dark shadow by his side, a specter that mocks him in the moonlight.

Time passes. Somehow, F keeps on living. He doesn't know how.

It is the next Christmas and F is going to church, father and mother sitting in the front of the car, F in the back.

F knows she will be there. Otherwise he wouldn't have come. He wants to see her one last time.

Just once.

They enter the sandstone church and find a place up the back. The regulars sit up front. Father gazes down at his hands. He too is enduring a sort of torture.

F sees Miranda sitting up front, with her mother. There is also a boy sitting beside her. A boy of the town, someone her mother approves of.

F channels his thoughts towards Miranda, willing her to turn around.

Instinctively she does so. The magic!

Her first expression is one of shock, but then there is the smile. The boy beside her also turns around to see who she is smiling at. He is properly dressed. The boy shoots F a dismissive look. F repays him with a murderous glare. The boy doesn't look at F again, for he sees that F would like to destroy him, and who knows, may even be up to doing just that, being from up the top end of the valley, up there in the wild.

The service is over. The people file out and gather out front. The women gossip earnestly beneath their flowery hats. The men engage in taciturn talk of cattle-prices and droughts.

F sees Miranda. She is with the other girls. She keeps looking in his direction.

He acts.

He strides over to her. The other girls immediately disappear.

"I hoped you'd come," she says.

His heart leaps! How could this be? His deathly existence just shot out the window in a matter of seconds?

His voice is low and steady,

"I love you Miranda."

She looks at him with laughter in her eyes, the laughter from before.

"I brought you this," she says, and hands him a book.

"What is it?" he asks, dazed.

"It's a bible of course!"

F stares blankly at the bible and then back at her.

"There is a letter inside of it," she says. "Take it home and read it."

At that moment Miranda's mother comes over. The mother gives F a suspicious glare.

"Come now dear, it's time we were going."

"Goodbye," says Miranda.

And then she is gone.

Driving back up the valley F is no longer aware of the plume of dust that was once such a source of fascination.

As the car careens up the road he opens the bible and takes out the letter. He reads. He cannot believe it. He reads again, and then lets his eyes rest on the horizon, deep in thought.

That night he takes the bible and the letter and goes up to the cave. He takes whisky. F lights a fire and takes a drink and then opens the bible and the letter. He reads slowly and steadily, re-reading line after line.

He studies each letter and imagines her writing the words and smells the paper just to grasp anything of her.

"I have special feelings for you but we need to live by the teachings of the Lord…

"I have sent you this bible so that you may begin to live according to Him…
"I have underlined special passages of importance for you to read…
"You know I always felt for you but we need to learn to put Him first…
"Yours in Christ, Miranda…"

F drinks.

The flames dance once more on the sandstone and the paintings leap with the flicker. He scrutinizes the night sky and senses the vastness of the universe. He drinks again and then he sets fire to the letter, watching the flames climbing up the curling paper, turning the words to ash. Then he weeps.

F drinks deeply now and stands at the opening of the cave. It is now the darkest hour. He releases a howl of anguish.

And the old spirits nod in approval. For the howl is that of life itself.

F packs his bags. He finds it intolerable to stay any longer. There is no question of his staying.

F leaves a note for his parents. He doesn't want to witness their repine.

In solitude he makes his way down the road. F is forthright in his movements. He has grown tall and strong on the land. He is well-framed.

Now his mind grows firm as well.

He passes the school without a glance. He stops at Miranda's gate and looks up to her house. All of the lights are out. There is no-one about.

F opens his bag and takes out the bible and places it in the mailbox. He leaves no note.

And then he is gone, gone, on down the road.

CHAPTER FIVE

The Old Man and the Hummingbird Have a Chat

"Tchiv, tchiv. Tchiv, tchiv."

"What is that sound?" wondered the old man. "First it is to my left, then in an instant to my right. Now it is above my head and suddenly far away. Could diabolical spirits be toying with my mind?"

"Tchiv, tchiv."

"But of course!" said the old man. "It is the hummingbird, for who else could move so far so fast?"

"Correct!" tchived the bird in his ear, before rocketing away.

"But hummingbird," said the old man. "It is only early in the spring. The flowers are but babes. What will you feed upon?"

"Old man, I can feed on the sap of a tree, so forfeit me your concern. I have come early for the jousting."

"The what?"

"The jousting!" chirruped the hummingbird, now from the far end of the garden.

"Oh, I see," said the old man. "But where is your competition?"

"Well isn't that precisely the point old man?" chipped the little bird, now inches from his nose, its body as still as a stone between whirring wings. "Only the strong survive, which kind of makes your survival a minor miracle! There ain't no second prize in my game, sir, and I can tell you that for nuttin. So when they come, I'll be ready."

The hummingbird rose vertically into the treetops and called out, "Come on then ya bastards! I'm ready for ya! I'll take the lot of ya!"

He descended again to the face of the old man.

"Just check me out," he laughed, holding his body side-on to the old man. "I'm irresistible!"

"Goodness me," said the old man. "You *are* an impressive sight. Your flanks are like some magical green metal and your throat sports a ruby cravat. I dare say you will be quite a hit with the ladies. Providing, that is, that you win the jousting."

"Ha! Don't you worry about that," sang the hummingbird as it skirted the jasmine. "Why do you think I move so fast, so early?"

"Truly little hummingbird, no bigger than my thumb, you do indeed move as creatures should, now here, now there, now up, now down, searching, exploring, yearning for contest and challenge and the prizes beyond."

"Movement is the key!" laughed the bird.

"Yes," said the old man. "Movement is noble because it is the natural way. To move is to expand both outwards and inwards. Movement is food for our inquisitiveness, and how our stomachs rumble with hunger!

"They are starving for truth!

CHAPTER SIX

The Wasp Returns

"Excuse my interrupting," said the wasp, with a sneer. "But how sorry for you, old man, for you cannot move! Thus, if movement leads to truth, then that is something you shall never attain. Instead, you exist at the mercy of my whim. Does this not weigh heavily upon you? For I have again caught you making presumptive claims, rich in pomposity."

"Ah, my dear wasp," said the old man. "Good morning!"

"Don't think for one moment that turning on the charm with civilities will save you," retorted the wasp, angrily. "You will have to do much more than that!

"But, dear me," continued the wasp, dripping with sarcasm, "I had forgotten. Who am I to talk? For are you not the greatest of men?"

"If the sun said so, then it must be so."

"You are a fraud old man," mocked the wasp. "For you didn't move to find truth. You moved to escape! To escape from your love that was lost."

"Wasp, I did run, it is true. I moved fast, like the hummingbird. But I did not run from a love lost so much as the opposite. I ran away from lies, in search of truth. I explored the corners of the globe and scaled the highest peaks. I swam flooded rivers and crossed oceans and deserts.

"And I did it all for truth."

"Bah!" spat the wasp. "An easy way out. You are a liar old man."

"My dear wasp," said the old man. "Do you not observe the world around you? Is not everything, including the ground below and the stars above, in constant flux and movement? Is movement not the rule? Just look at the babe asleep on the mother's back, content in movement, but crying as soon as it is laid still."

"But just look at you men of today," said the wasp. "Men of today deride movement. They are sedentary beasts. What has happened to your brethren?"

The old man sighed.

"Ever since men moved away from their original state, and learnt how to control water and grow grain and make beasts dumb, and built towns and cities, they ceased to move. Yet even those men acknowledged that in their grand design they had lost something pure and had soiled themselves.

"For did not the nomads of the desert look down upon sedentary men with scorn? And did not the men of the cities send their sons to live with the nomads? For the nomadic life was always considered the noble life, the clean life, and the upright and natural life, the life of movement.

"And then, when the sons returned to the cities, they would often flee back to be with the nomads in a sort of horrific comprehension of what men had done to themselves."

"Old man, I can see you are beginning to ramble in your senility. So focus now! I don't require some dinner-party prattle. I require a story. Speak to me now of movement. And speak well for my tail itches!"

CHAPTER SEVEN

The Second Story

It was difficult for F to pin-point exactly when it all began, when the spark was first lit, but he usually associated it with the book.

One could be forgiven for thinking it was the boyhood trips to England to meet the far-off relatives whom he neither knew nor could pretend to care much for. The aged grandma that drank sherry and said, "Shh, don't tell your mother."

There was the spectacle of Trafalgar Square, with the pigeons and the towering outline of Nelson atop his column, flanked by the façade of the National Gallery and all of the treasures within. F seeing 'Sunflowers' by Van Gogh, yet still young enough to say, in complete innocence, "Mum, I prefer the pictures where the women have no clothes on."

There was the ominous and foreboding Tower of London, with its white stone walls and ravens that must never leave or the towers will surely fall, where the beefeaters strolled by the chopping block where queens had lost their heads.

There were also parades outside Buckingham Palace, F too small to see through the massed crowds, climbing a fountain to catch a glimpse above the multitude, only to be chastised by a bobby. There was the changing of the guards, their expressions immoveable as granite beneath their buzz-bees.

F was overwhelmed by the vast dome of St. Paul's, the name of Christopher Wren forever etched in his mind. He marveled at the Tower Bridge, spanning the Thames beneath constant grey skies, and was enthralled by the sight of jellied eels, a delicacy that harked back to the medieval times, and to the times before that.

Strange wonders.

And on his return journey to Australia, being in Singapore, hit by the tropical humidity as if by an invisible and incalculable wall, gazing in amazement as night fires were lit in the streets for religious festivals and snakes were hung in restaurant windows or writhed in buckets down in Chinatown, F standing there, his jaw agape, stunned by the smells of chicken feet and pig hooves and tongues and brains and other chthonic animal parts.

Or perhaps it was not so much the things he saw, but that they were different and new?

But in order to see and smell and taste the different and the new, one had to *move*.

For even then, at that young age, F's heart leapt in excitement as the plane's wheels left the tarmac and the fuselage shuddered.

F would stare for hours at the world far below, down at vast oceans and deserts where the sight of a boat or any human life would make his heart jump. As they flew through the night he would look at the stars and *feel* higher up, like he was *with* the stars, *in* the universe, with its baffling vastness and bewildering eternity.

But back to the book.

It was really the book that did it. *Afghanistan*. Quite a small book really. Mostly photographs of people in bazaars, a river flowing serenely through the verdure of Kabul, the mighty Hindu Kush soaring on the horizon, the very name, 'Hindu Kush' or 'Hindu Killer' indelibly imprinted in his thoughts.

Then there was the green and fertile Bamiyan Valley. Ah, how that picture filled him with delight, with the giant Buddhas carved into the cliff faces, overlooking the poplar-lined roads that ran through the fields. How even at that young age, F didn't just want to go there. He also wanted to *live* there and he sensed already the cool air and the smell of pomegranates as he looked down from his house on the mountainside.

F wanted to *live* there. He even felt that he already had.

And just as striking to F were the pictures of the lakes in the Pamir Mountains further north, with astonishing blues and greens, those mountains giving birth to the mighty Oxus River that descended to dissect the boundless deserts of Central Asia, expanses blistered and crumpled beneath an interminable weight of heat for an immeasurable eon.

And why had the name Krasnovodsk reverberated so powerfully with F? Was it because the railway to the Caspian Sea terminated there? Yes! F yearned to take *that* train.

F itched for adventure.

Atreo and F both woke late. It was Fatima the maid who had knocked gently on F's door and entered with his breakfast on a silver tray. On her way out she picked up his dirty clothes and carried them away to launder. F sank back in the feather pillows and drank coffee and reveled in his situation. His room was enormous. Outside the rain poured down.

Fatima returned to take the tray and ran F a bath. He bathed and shaved and put on his clothes and went out to the sitting room. F read the papers in an enormous leather chair and drank coffee and smoked cigarettes.

He felt absolutely sublime.

"How on earth have I ended up here?" he thought to himself. *"What a twist of fate. Months of sleeping on beaches for lack of money and now this!"*

His eyes ran over the antique furniture and dark wood and the Persian carpets and silverware. He was in an apartment, an extraordinary apartment, situated in a grand old building in downtown Madrid. The Prado was a stone's throw away, as was the Plaza Major. And on top of all that he was washed and cleaned and fed. Why wouldn't he feel absolute happiness after all of the months of slumming it?

He drew on his cigarette and drank the coffee.

F recalled the events of the previous evening. He arrived at Madrid Airport in the rain, hardly a cent to his name, just armed with a phone number for Atreo, arriving without any warning, just in the blind hope that Atreo would be there to save his neck, not even considering what to do if Atreo *weren't* there, just telling himself that Atreo *would* be there. And sure enough, Atreo had answered the phone and within thirty minutes had arrived in a chauffeur driven limo, and then they were carving through the streets of Madrid.

"My God F, you look like a hobo! You look like you've been sleeping on beaches!"

"I *have* been sleeping on beaches."

"Well, however that may be," said Atreo with the natural confidence borne of aristocracy, "you cannot meet my parents looking like *that*. We will go in the back and you can bathe and put on one of my suits. Oh my God!" he said, with his booming laugh. "You look like a bum!"

F was bundled in through the rear entrance and bathed and dressed before he had time to get his bearings. He had been flung headfirst into another world.

They entered the dining room where Atreo's parents were already seated. F was formally introduced as "a fellow scholar of archaeology".

F glanced nervously at the father. He was old, militaristic and craggy. His eyes were stern. The mother was high-society.

As Fatima approached with the dishes, F felt that she would stumble at any moment, so paralyzed with fear did she seem to be around the father.

Atreo, thankfully, was as polished and charming as ever.

"I think you will like this wine," he said. "It is from a vineyard owned by my family in Portugal."

F read the label and recognized parts of Atreo's full name,

'Atreo de Toledo.'

F felt like such a dunce. There he was in Spain and, quite frankly, he didn't know the very first thing about the place. He couldn't even speak a word of Spanish to save himself. He had even been lectured to on the plane by the lady in the next seat. As they had landed, F had looked out of the window and said "Madrid". The lady had grabbed his arm and informed him in no uncertain terms, "No, No, No, No! Not *Madrid*. It is *Madridth*!"

F had no clue about the history of Spain and was even unaware that there had been a civil war and that Atreo's father had served with Franco and had seen the hard edge of those times. And if F had also seen those times, then he too would never smile but would only snarl out orders. F didn't know what a Basque was or even a Catalan. And he had no idea that when Madrid played Barcelona in football it was not just a game but a further extension of war.

And when Fatima brought the silver platter with the fish to his elbow, F's embarrassment was paramount, for he had never been *served* a fish before. And not only that, he had hardly ever even eaten a fish before, so had no concept of how to *take* part of a fish, especially under the scrutinizing gaze of the father. F was convinced that Atreo's parents considered him a cultural Neanderthal.

Which, in a sense, he was.

But, thankfully, dinner was short. Atreo took F off to the drawing room and procured a bottle of Iberian firewater. The rain continued to pour. It was November.

They drank and Atreo took F to another room where he kept his collection of military uniforms. And with the drinking, they each put on uniforms with the boots and caps and swords and leapt about the apartment, sword fighting and laughing.

Then, when it was late, they were driven to a tapas bar, still wearing their uniforms. They met up with Atreo's friends, archaeology-types mostly. There had been more bars and a party and someone had slipped F a pill, which he took, but which seemed to have little effect, so overwhelmed was F with just being there.

And in the wee hours Atreo and F were stumbling about in the shadows. A man stepped towards them and pulled out a knife. F flew into a fury at the affront and cursed him for being a coward and dared him to fight like a man, hand to hand. As the man took another step towards him, knife held out straight, F whipped out his sword, which flashed in the light of the streetlamps. As soon as the sword was out the man was gone, F swearing blue murder and baying for blood.

Atreo quickly led F away.

"You must be very careful of these men. They are Arabs. It is a big problem here."

Danger.

F felt it everywhere. But he was young and of indomitable spirit and still possessing the most sincere belief of youth in its own immortality.

Danger was everywhere. Why, it had even been there when F had met Atreo back in Israel six months prior. It had been there when F had ended up in *that* situation in the Sinai. And also when he had been drugged and robbed on the beach in Tel Aviv.

But somehow, F not only got through it all, but was exhilarated by it and thrived on it.

The omnipresence of danger was nowhere more evident than with the Israeli archaeologists on the excavation, who believed that the whole world was out to get them. The excavation itself, in the far north of the country, below the Golan Heights and bordering the Lebanon, also had an odor of danger just through sheer location. F was never comfortable when they went for a 'relaxing' swim in the

Golan Heights, amidst the bullet-riddled houses and bomb craters and barbed wire.

As far as F was concerned there was nothing 'relaxing' about it.

On the excavation, the Israelis kept to themselves. So too did the Americans from the evangelical university. It was just as well that they didn't mix, such was F's distaste for them, with their bible-studies and virginal prayers.

But then there were the Spaniards.

Thank God for the Spaniards. They represented the bacchanalian streak, whipping up vats of sangria and dancing the flamenco, the girls being of a stunning beauty with eyes that sparkled with suggestion, singing of passion and love beneath the pine trees in the moonlight.

"I wish I spoke Spanish," F said to Atreo, looking at the girls.

"Ah yes!" replied Atreo, with a twinkle in his eye. "But there is one language that everyone speaks!"

Every night F was with the Spaniards, who adopted him as one of their own and were, in a way, fascinated by F, he being from the other side of the earth, from a land undreamt of and far beyond their comprehension.

But where was there more danger and excitement than in Jerusalem, at the epicenter of the poisonous fumes from the crack in the rock?

F had made his way there and gone through the Damascus Gate and the white walls of Suleiman and into the chaos of the Arab Quarter. He could not afford to stay in the Christian or Jewish or Armenian Quarters. He walked up a dirty flight of stairs of a hostel. A fat Arab with long and curly, oily hair, sat behind the desk.

"You call me *Abu*," he said.

F recoiled.

"Isn't *Abu* Arabic for *Father*?" he asked angrily. "Is that your thing you dirty bastard? You want all these fresh-faced Europeans to call you *Daddy*?"

The Arab flung his head back with a roaring laugh.

"Oh my God!" he exclaimed. "You got it! For you, the first night is free!"

F looked around. There was a grimy courtyard with open showers. Backpackers sat around in groups, playing backgammon and smoking cigarettes. He looked inside. The rooms were rank, creaking bunks of rust with bug-infested foam mattresses, stained with the sweat and fluids of a thousand and one travelers.

F went up to the roof and threw his pack down. He kept an eye on it these days, what with all that had happened.

The Old City crowded around him. He could clearly see the Temple Mount and the Dome of the Rock and the Al-Aqsa Mosque. Up the slope loomed the grey church of the Holy Sepulcher and Golgotha. The air hummed with frenzied tension.

He went downstairs.

A tall man with very fair hair arrived and announced in a loud voice,

"I like Hitler!"

Once more the fat Arab boomed out his laugh.

"For you, my friend, the first night is free!"

F was sitting with Peer, playing chess, smoking and drinking. Peer looked dismissively at the other backpackers, and said, quite loudly, and most certainly deliberately, "Just take a look at these imbeciles playing backgammon! What a ridiculous game! A game for monkeys."

Grumbles could be heard but no one really wanted to stand up to Peer and make an issue out of it. Peer was too big, too strong, but there was also something about his ingrained arrogance that they feared.

Peer swung back to F as if nothing had happened.

"Honestly, why are they even here? They have no interest in anything around them. They just play that stupid game that depends on luck."

Peer frowned, but then perked up.

"So, you have a farm you say? What does your family have its money in? Sheep? How many? Fifty thousand? One hundred thousand?"

Peer had not said this to poke fun at F. He was sincere in his questions, for he, like Atreo, was also from one of those aristocratic European worlds where wealth knew no bounds.

"I have just had it with these Israelis," Peer said. "They are the most intolerable people on earth, and the most racist."

F was bemused by the claim.

He related to Peer all of the misfortunes he had experienced in Sinai and Tel Aviv.

"Yep, I'm outta here tomorrow," F said. "I'm going to Cyprus by ferry. Good bloody riddance."

Peer leant in.

"I have an idea."

Later that evening, F and Peer were sitting in a very good restaurant in the Jewish New City. They were dining alfresco. Peer was ordering the wine, of which he seemed to have an expansive knowledge. F was only aware of there being red and white.

They drank heavily, F patiently listening to Peer and his anti-Semitic rants, as they ordered the most expensive dishes on the menu.

"Skoal!" exclaimed Peer, with a smile. "This one is on Abraham's kin!"

Then, when coffee was ordered and the waiter had gone back inside, Peer and F upped and bolted through the streets of the New City.

Behind them were loud yells and the sounds of waiters giving chase, but Peer and F were both young and strong and flying high and pretty much unstoppable at that point.

Sirens were sounding now, coming and going, but Peer and F cut through the backstreets, fast, back to the haven of the Arab Quarter, for no Israeli would go into such a place after dark. And there was also the half-hope that the sirens were for something else, for there was always trouble somewhere in that benighted city.

Back in the safety of the hostel they drank on and on. Peer was soaring high, in a revelatory mood.

"That was great!" Peer whooped across the rooftops. "Now that, my friend, is what I would call high art!"

And they drank until F was alone on the roof, on his hands and knees, being sick, heaving and breathing hard, the world about him spinning. And his head ached as though crowned with thorns and the air was thick with the history of strife and horror and massacres and wars.

F's head thumped with the pulsing heartbeat of doom. Names flew by in a torrent just as blood had flowed in the streets below, Canaanites and Philistines and Jews and Edomites and Ammonites and Moabites and Amorites and Romans and Christians and Arabs and Persians and Crusaders and Turks.

And in that state, more akin to a retching dog than a man, eyes agog and his face wet with sweat, F felt Jerusalem close in on him and as if he was in the guts of hell.

But F was moving.

CHAPTER EIGHT

The Old Man and the Wasp Speak of Art

"Moving?" laughed the wasp, now seated on the shoulder of the old man. "The only thing moving were your bowels! And even they were going in the wrong direction. Ha! You call that a story? Not a trace of linear action or character development! That was deserving of my sting!"

"Why wasp!" exclaimed the old man. "You speak like a literary critic. Perhaps you missed your calling?"

"Don't tempt me old man. That story was here, there and everywhere. And where were you searching for your truth anyway? Did you find it on the blood-drenched streets of Jerusalem?"

The old man laughed.

"I like that little wasp, 'the blood-drenched streets of Jerusalem'. You may have the poet in you yet!"

"Old man!" yelled the wasp. "Don't tempt me! Spring is here and in full swing. I am at my most virile and am bursting for action. I feel as though my venom can barely be contained!"

"Less haste, little wasp, for I gave you what you asked for.

"For the story moved as life moves - now here, now there, now behind you, now in front, without beginning, without end. But truth is elusive and movement is an art."

"Oho! An art! And you are a great artist too no doubt?" mocked the wasp.

"Forgive me, little wasp, I misspoke. To attempt to speak of art is mere foolishness."

"So speak of art then, fool," commanded the wasp.

"Art is everything and nothing and all in between."

"What? Are these the words of infirmity?"

"No. Art is creation and creation is life and life is all."

"What!" scoffed the wasp, "Even a wasp knows that art is to be found in a drawing or a painting or a sculpture?"

"No wasp. Art is the most ambiguous of terms, for art means all things to all men."

"So it would seem old man, that you have a tricky task before you!"

"And what," asked the old man, "is that?"

"Speak to me of art and do so well, for if you fail I will teach you the art of dying."

CHAPTER NINE

The Third Story

Mariette was a Belgian, but she considered herself French.

She was from the south of the country, the Francophone south, and therefore, by right, as if pre-ordained by the greatness of the powers that be, she also considered herself to be 'artistic'.

She told F in no uncertain terms what she thought of him being an Australian.

"You see the problem with you Australians is that you have no culture. You are not artistic."

Despite F's dislike of Mariette, there was simply no ignoring the fact that she had the best legs on the whole archaeological expedition.

F had seen them, because, much to the expedition director's chagrin, she insisted on playing barefoot soccer with the local Arab boys. She would hold her skirt up high as she ran, and the boys spent more time gaping at her legs than looking at the ball.

The director frowned.

"F will you go out there and stop that bloody crazy French broad before the mullah arrives. Jesus. Doesn't she know anything?"

F ambled out onto the plateau above the Jordan River Valley. He called over to Mariette.

"What?" she said, breathing hard, her high cheekbones flushed, her eyes the grey of a wolf.

"You have to stop," said F.

"Why?" she replied, hands on hips.

"Word will get around about us infidels and there will be problems. You can't go around here showing your legs like that. It will raise the ire of the imam."

"Screw you!" she said, lividly. "You know what your problem is? You Australians are all racists. It's ridiculous that I can't play football with the boys."

"Well, don't come running to me if the locals want to stone you to death," said F, half-hoping they would.

But at other times, F had come across Mariette when she was quite calm and content, sitting and sketching. Mariette had been brought out to draw the small-finds on the excavation, the pottery and the coins and the figurines. But she spent most of her time outside, sketching camels, or the local boys, or the landscape. It was certainly picturesque there in Jordan, looking out across the river valley, rural, idyllic.

F looked at her pictures.

They were nearly all charcoal on paper. F didn't think they were all that good but considered it prudent to remain silent on the matter.

Despite F's dislike of Mariette he agreed to accompany her to Syria. The truth of the matter was that his instincts were brutally base. He could clearly remember Jock cornering him at the Institute in Amman.

"You're going to shag her right? You're going to shag her aren't you ya canny lad!"

"Oh, I don't think so," said F, dishonestly.

"Bullshit! She's a fine looking lassie! You've seen the legs. And she's a bloody artist! You know what they're all like, they'll shag at the drop of a hat. No morals. Perfect!"

F could also remember looking out the bus window as they drove out of town and how Mariette had smiled and waved happily to the men outside the mosque and how they had called back with curses, and she, not speaking Arabic, not realizing the meaning of their words, turned to F and said, "You see, they are the friendliest people on earth. You are no more than a stupid racist."

F had grimaced as he turned away.

F planned on staying in Damascus and again felt that old thrill as they roared across the fertile plains of the Hauran, the grand white peaks of the Lebanon visible in the distance, towards that most ancient and wondrous of cities.

But once the taxi arrived at the depot Mariette was adamant that they must head straight for Tartus, on the coast.

"Are you insane?" exclaimed F. "You've never even been in Damascus before. You *have* to see it. You can't just turn up here and leave. You'd be out of your mind."

"I am going to Tartus," said Mariette defiantly. "And you are coming? I thought we agreed that you would travel with me? What has changed?"

F looked at her amber hair glimmer in the late afternoon Damascene light.

"Ah shit," he said. "It's you that's missing out. Let's go to bloody Tartus then."

"There is no need to act like that," Mariette scoffed. "I need to see the ocean. You wouldn't understand because you don't have a romantic bone in your body. Have you ever been to Tartus?"

"No."

"Then we're even," she declared triumphantly, as she headed off in search of the bus.

The following evening they were dining on the shores of the Mediterranean, eating fish caught straight out of the boat.

It had been a magnificent day. To the south, the snow-capped mountains of the Lebanon dropped straight into the sea. Off to the north, the coast stretched to the Syrian Gates and Cilicia. The sky was a gentle blue and the sun dropped gloriously over the horizon, off between the Pillars of Hercules, off beyond the compass. The island of Arvad was outlined in silhouette just off-shore.

The whole 'art' thing had come up again.

"So tell me then," said F. "What exactly is art to you anyway?"

Mariette showed him her sketch book the way a teacher would show a picture-book to a child.

She had drawn a camel.

"So what," said F. "You're not the first person to draw a camel? And I'm sure there have been much better camels drawn a thousand times over."

Mariette ground her teeth.

"My God. You are so offensive! Art is creation. I have created this camel. I am a creator!"

"But if art is creativity then it has to be something *new*."

"Are you blind?" she exclaimed, prodding the book with her forefinger. "*This* is new. *This* is creation."

"So if I throw paint at a canvas that would be creativity thus it would also be art?"

"Yes," she sighed.

F took a drink and lit a cigarette. A few minutes passed.

"I think its bullshit," he said, disparagingly.

"What?" she gasped, incredulously.

"No less than nonsensical garbage."

Mariette was speechless.

"Well, then," she said, trying to control her rage. "Do you have any other opinions you would like to share? Tell me something else about art?"

"I saw 'Sunflowers' when I was a boy."

Mariette broke out laughing.

"OK then," she said, crossing her legs and leaning back. "What did you think of Sunflowers?"

"You have a great pair of legs you know," said F.

Mariette ignored the comment.

"Sunflowers?" she demanded.

"It's alright."

"Alright?" she burst out. "Alright? Are you out of your mind?"

"No. I preferred the naked ladies though."

"God. OK then, are there any impressionists that you *do* like?"

"Renoir and Cezanne."

"What! We agree!" she said, clapping her hands to her cheeks. "I cannot believe it!"

Mariette filled their glasses.

"Cheers!"

"Cheers!"

F smiled.

"But I have to tell you," he said, leaning in. "There is something else about impressionism."

"Oh yes," she said, eyes flashing.

"Perhaps it would be best if I didn't say," said F, sitting back.

"Oh! Now I *have* to know!"

"No. It would just set you off on one of your Gallic tantrums."

Mariette snapped bolt upright. F envisioned a wild Belgian tribeswoman before him.

"Explain yourself!" she commanded.

"I think impressionism is basically bullshit."

"Go on," she said savagely.

"Well, the problem is that the medium of paint was pushed as far as it would go. After realism had reached its apex painters had to search to find something new to create, and Renoir and Cezanne discovered something special. But that development was like the flash of a supernova, and ever since then painting has degenerated, for there was nowhere else for it to go."

Mariette huffed and looked out to sea.

He thought he had better let it go, but Mariette took up the reins once more.

"What about Picasso then? What about the Cubists? What about Kandinsky?"

"Garbage."

"Well," sighed Mariette, taking a sip and glancing out across the sunset. "Your views are certainly unconventional. Tell me then, how do you rank the arts?"

F thought for a while.

"I have met architects who considered their art to be ranked highest, even if all they have created is an apartment block that is no more than a box full of boxes. Architecture used to be one of the great arts. But it has gone the way of all modern art, descending into vacuity, bereft of any real meaning."

"Then who are the highest artists?"

"The highest artists are musicians. They are higher than painters and poets, for they can conjure up images through music, that most heavenly gift, that highest language that laughs in the face of our words. Music can draw out powerful emotions unlike any of the other arts.

"Truly, I tell you that music, the unspoken language that is common to us all, that moves us all, is the only realm where the artist and audience become entwined in a theurgic state, where the audience becomes the chorus in the original sense of the term. It is then that Dionysius reveals himself.

"Blessed are the musical."

That night they each got in their own beds. They had candles for light. F looked at Mariette.

"Do you want to sleep together?"

Mariette turned over and stared at him in disbelief.

"Do I look like I want to have sex with you? I don't think I even like you."

Mariette turned back over and went to sleep and F lay there for a time, feeling sort of embarrassed and stupid.

The following morning they had breakfast and walked down to the water-front. They took a boat out to Arvad and looked around at the ruins. Mariette kept 'oohing' and 'aahing' over the souvenirs that were for sale.

F couldn't have given a brass razoo for souvenirs.

They went into a tea-house, full of men, local fishermen mostly.

Mariette began sketching a gnarly old fisherman with a weather-beaten, grey whiskered face.

Soon, all the other men gathered around as the old fisherman sat immobile, aware that he was being sketched.

The picture went from bad to worse. It was almost as if the longer Mariette sketched the uglier she made him look.

The other men kept laughing and calling out to him in Arabic, "Ha ha! You have a face like a donkey's bum!"

Finally, the old fisherman could wait no longer. Mariette showed him the picture. He angrily denounced it as "rubbish!"

On the boat back to Tartus, Mariette was enraged.

"It's not my fault that he looks that way. He just needs to accept the facts!"

Then F let her have it.

"Perhaps you just need to accept that you're not a very good artist?"

Mariette gripped the rails of the boat, her knuckles white.

She turned to him, her hair snapping viciously in the wind.

"When we get to land I suggest you go to Damascus and I head my own way," she hissed through gritted teeth.

F said nothing. It clearly had to happen.

F got his things and headed on down to the depot for the bus to Damascus. He felt enormously relieved to be free of Mariette.

He then heard footsteps running up behind him.

"Wait! Just wait!" she called.

F stared at her. She really was quite beautiful when she was flushed.

"I'll wait for the bus with you."

"OK," said F, indifferently.

They found a table in a chaikana and sat down and lit cigarettes.

Mariette exhaled with an air of extreme frustration.

"Look," she said. "I feel bad. I know we don't exactly 'get on'. I think we should travel apart as planned. But you're really not all that bad. At least we can end this as friends, you know, from an honest perspective."

"Fine," replied F.

Mariette smiled.

"You really are a very beautiful girl you know," he said.

"Why didn't you say that before?"

"I didn't think I needed to. I thought it was obvious."

"But what on earth were you doing wanting to have sex with me? What was that all about?"

"Well, you do like to have sex, right?"

"Yes."

"Well, so do I. We should have screwed."

"Pah," she laughed. "You are such a Neanderthal. But at least you are an intelligent one. I may not like the things you say, and what you said to me was very mean, but at least you have an opinion."

"Well. I'm sorry. What I said *was* mean."

"Apology accepted."

"But you must admit that you can be the most infuriating bitch?"

Mariette froze and glared at F, but then it left her and she smiled again.

"I still think you are wrong about art," she threw down again with a challenge.

F laughed.

"I think that any opinion held on art is ridiculous. Art is an ambiguous term that holds different meanings for different people. It's like cheese or wine or poetry. One person will like something and consider it worthy of the term. Another will consider it nonsense. Any definition of the term is completely subjective.

"The real problem lies in our inability to convey what we really mean. We are prisoners of our own grammar. We speak in a language of arbitrary terms. We are mere babes in the woods and it is a miracle we can understand each other at all."

Mariette leaned back in her chair. F gave her a good looking up and down.

"Sure you don't want to?" he said with a grin.
She laughed.

"God! Seriously, tell me, you don't really think Picasso is rubbish do you?"

"Yes."

"Amazing. What about Dali?"

"Dali? I didn't think he was 'cool' among you serious artistic types?"

"He had his moments," she said.

"I'll tell you a story about Dali," said F. "When he was a boy he would climb into a tower in the countryside and would spy down upon the peasant women as they picked oranges in the orchards and he would masturbate!"

"Oh dear," said Mariette. "Maybe you should go after all. Look here is your bus."

The bus rumbled up to a stop.

Mariette leant in and kissed F on the cheek.

"So no hard feelings then?" she said softly.

"None," said F.

Mariette smiled.

"This is just life. It is better we go our own ways. But I want to do so with honesty."

"Yes," replied F. "We are hard on each other. But we are honest with each other, and that is rare."

Mariette stared out to sea. F leant in and whispered in her ear,

"*Music is the highest art but honesty is the rarest art.*"

Back at the Institute in Amman, F sat down at the desk while Jock opened a bottle of whisky and smiled charmingly. He pushed a glass over to F and said in his broad brogue, "Well?"

"Well what?"

"Don't play canny with me laddie! You know damn well what?"

"What?"

"I want to hear what happened. Was she a good shag?"

"Oh!" F laughed. "No, I didn't shag her."

Jock stared at him in blatant disbelief.

"What the hell do ya mean laddie?" he roared. "Of course ye shagged her."

"No, really, I didn't shag her."

"I don't believe you."

"Nope. Didn't happen."

"You're lying."

"Nope."

"You're lying."

"Nope"

Jock sat back heavily in his chair, gravely disappointed. Minutes passed as they sipped their drinks.

Then Jock looked at F again with the fire in his eye.

"You're lying."

Summer

CHAPTER TEN

The Old Man and the Wasp Meet Again

"So at least one man knew you were a liar?" said the wasp, acidly.

"Dear me, are you always in such a foul mood?" asked the old man.

"It is the first lick of summer. It makes me irritable," responded the wasp.

"Ah," sighed the old man. "Mariette would have made a good match for you. She too had an overabundance of venom."

"Quiet! Desist! It is I that is meant to sting you and not you me. Your words are a constant barrage of tiny barbs and lies that sap my strength and patience."

The old man pretended to be offended.

"Lies? Am I to be accused of being a liar when I was telling the truth? Is it not a cruel irony that I get called a cheat when I speak honestly?"

"You were meant to speak about art, not about honesty," hissed the wasp.

"And there was a difference? For is not honesty an art?"

"Old man be warned! Your thoughts are dribbling like your dinner down your shirt."

"Dear wasp, truth is there and waits to be found, but skills must be acquired along the way. Honesty is the mightiest of swords, but one most difficult to obtain. It is fixed in a stone on the summit of a mountain of thorns. One gets cut and poisoned if one attempts to reach it. Most choose not to do so."

"Thorns? Ha! Your mind is a briar patch of cob-webbed illusions," mocked the wasp.

"No wasp. I chose to fight my way through the brambles and climb up through the thorns to win the sword, and I was cut and I bled profusely. But I moved and I *learned* honesty, for through no other means could the sword be gained! I *learned* that rarest of arts.

"And I tell you this, such an achievement was no easy task. On my quest I had to partake of the most sickening draughts from the most sinister vials."

"More vile than my venom?" threatened the wasp.

"Your venom is but a cordial compared to the poisons of which I speak."

The wasp darted upon the nose of the old man and raised its tail.

"Old man, I will be the judge of that! Tell me now, of what poisons did you drink to win your famed sword?"

CHAPTER ELEVEN

The Fourth Story

Keith was from London and was wearing a Westham United shirt.

"Come on you 'ammers. Come on you 'ammers," he yelled after a few beers.

Keith took a toke on a scraggly joint. He was as brown as a nut. He spent his days sun-bathing, covered in coconut oil. To an Englishman, having a tan is a magnificent novelty.

"Yeah mate, what more could you want that this?" he asked.

"Keith, I have to tell you I'm kind of bored here?" said F.

Keith looked at F in stunned disbelief.

"How could you be bored?" he exclaimed. "We are in heaven! It's sunny and hot every day. You are on the ocean and can swim. You are surrounded by endless pussy. And you can smoke pot anywhere. God, what a great place! Come on 'ammers!"

"But aren't you fed up with all the goddam reggae music?" said F. "Jesus, it never stops."

Another stunned silence.

At that moment Jerome, a very tall and lanky Sudanese arrived with a bag of pot for Keith.

Keith beamed.

"Yo Jerome my man, what's up?"

Keith handed Jerome his joint for a toke.

"Yo Keith, jus chillun man."

Jerome languidly sauntered off with the joint. F frowned.

"And what's with everyone speaking like they are from Jamaica? Smoking pot and listening to reggae doesn't mean you're from bloody Jamaica. This is Sinai for crissakes! We're in Dahab, not Kingston. And Jerome is not some easy going Rasta. He's a bloody cut-throat Sudanese who'd knife you in the back for a buck."

Keith had begun to roll another joint.

"You know, you just need to chill man. Take it easy on Jerome. He's cool. Can't you just go and get laid?"

Maybe Keith was right? But why did F find it so tiresome to go through the rituals of chatting up girls? His thoughts kept turning to Sinai.

"What do you say Keith? Want to go and climb Mount Sinai?"

Keith looked at F like he had finally lost the plot.

"What? And leave all this?"

The taxi headed west into the blazing deserts of Sinai and wound through the mountains into a grand and formidable landscape, bleached white and stripped bare. In places the terrain opened up into flat yellow ghars, out of which black volcanic cones sprang up. F was mesmerized and transported with delight as he coasted through this mysterious landscape.

F began his ascent at Saint Catherine's Monastery. It was early afternoon and the path was wide and well-trodden, the rocks smoothed over or turned into the finest powdered dust by the countless feet of pilgrims.

After hours of climbing F stopped and looked about. He was high up. There was nothing around. Not a person, a house, a blade of grass, only the most stark and barren peaks, dried to their very cores.

As he continued on, F began to notice mounds of toilet paper accompanied by the pungent smell of feces, a shock after spending hours in the pure air of desert heights. As he neared the summit, the mounds of toilet paper grew in number until they veritably dotted the landscape. At the same time, the passing wafts mounted into a powerful and constant odor.

When F got to the summit, there was so much excrement that he had to watch where he stepped.

F found a slab of rock and opened his pack, ate some biscuits, drank some water, and waited. He looked around him. Other back-packers were arriving. To F's surprise there was a stone shack right on the very top, where an Arab sold bottles of water and sodas and packs of chips.

But one thing was for sure. There was no toilet.

Yet in spite of the crude and distasteful products of men, the work of nature that F beheld was forbidding and grand. The ridges dropped into a haze of twilight and the sun descended in bloody shades of crimson. The mountain peaks cast long, purple shadows deep into the timeless desert valleys far below.

"*How can desolation hold so much beauty?*" F wondered with awe.

F spread out his sleeping bag and lay on his back and smoked and lost himself in the stars that drifted above him. He thought about Moses and the Ten Commandments and fell into blessed oblivion and sleep.

When F awoke he was being trampled upon.

German and French and Italian voices made a terrible din in the darkness.

"What the hell!" he cursed.

The crowd continued by him without any pause. They selected the best vantage points for the sunrise and set up their tripods and programmed their cameras.

F sat up so that people could at least see him and not stomp all over him. He could make out a faint glow on the eastern horizon.

"Tourists," grumbled F, lighting a cigarette.

F did the calculations. It took four hours to climb Mount Sinai. Plus, a two hour coach ride from the nearest luxury hotel. Six hours. So they must have left at midnight.

Then, when the sun appeared, there was a blinding flash that set the desert ablaze with a phosphorescent white so powerful that it was painful to look at. The real beauty had been in the sunset.

At the same moment the air was punctuated by a cacophony of beeps and whirrs and clicks of expensive cameras.

"I've had enough of this," said F.

So he descended the mountain.

"How was Sinai?" asked Keith, in a stoned blur. "Did you see Moses or God up there or anything like that?"

"Nope. There was crap everywhere. Seriously. *Everywhere*. And also a lot of Germans."

"The Bosch? Well. Glad I didn't go then," said Keith, and handed F a smoke.

A little later F went back to his 'hotel room', an unlocked concrete block, and discovered that his camera was missing.

He recalled seeing Jerome dart away when he had entered the courtyard.

"That sonofabitch!" F cursed.

The police station was comprised of a single, white-washed room. The sole policeman of Dahab was leaning back in his chair, his feet on the desk. He was stoned to the eyeballs.

The policeman was onto a pretty good thing. Everyone in town did him favors in return for him turning a blind eye to any indiscretions. Wherever he went, he was given free meals, free drinks, and free pot.

"What do you want me to do?" he laughed.

"I want a statement so I can claim insurance," said F. "That's all. I don't actually expect to get my camera back."

The policeman just shrugged and laughed again. F could tell it was all a futile waste of time.

At that moment three very officious policemen entered the room. The local policeman remained stunned momentarily with his feet on the desk, before shooting up out of his chair and to attention. The three were from headquarters and conducting a surprise inspection.

F explained the situation.

There was an immediate flurry of activity. They all filed over to F's 'hotel', his room was inspected, the Sudanese were rounded up and then they were all piled together into the police jeep and roared off to headquarters.

In the jeep, the Sudanese shot F some sharp looks and muttered angrily to each other. They were looked down upon by the Egyptians and were not going to be cut any favors, at least not for a small price.

Jerome stared venomously at F.

"Why have you done this?" hissed Jerome.

"Done what?"

"Look at this situation you've put us in. This is no good."

F scowled at Jerome.

"If you weren't a thieving bastard none of this would have happened."

Jerome glared furiously at F.

"You are very stupid. We can make life very hard for you. You don't understand how it works around here. If this turns out bad for us, we will make it bad for you".

"Screw you," said F.

But he was nonetheless grateful for the presence of the armed police.

The regional headquarters were located some miles inland, well into the desert. The police took F's passport and told him to sit down on a bench. The Sudanese were placed in a cell, close to where F sat.

Men in uniform milled about, or sat drinking tea and smoking cigarettes. They seemed lethargic and disinterested in what they were doing, but each was shuffling or signing papers, or carrying papers from one room to another to shuffle them there or to get another signature. Each man wore an expression of bored resignation.

After all, what could be worse than being assigned to Dahab in the Sinai Desert, so far away from the follies of Cairo?

F approached the front desk. He observed his passport placed to the side.

"Sir," said the policeman behind the desk. "Please sit down. We have searched the hotel premises and have found much evidence of illegal activities."

F went and sat down.

Jerome moved over to the edge of the cell so that he was within whispering distance. He leant as close as he could and spat out, "You bastard, we are going to kill you when we get out of here. This doesn't look so good for us. When we get out you better be ready. We are going to stick you with a knife. Then you'll see."

The phone rang and the policeman at the desk picked it up and began a long, rambling conversation, swinging around in his chair with his back to F. The Sudanese were whispering amongst themselves and glaring at F.

F deftly got to his feet, swiftly approached the desk, and in a flash snatched up his passport and made for the exit. He kept waiting for cries of "stop", but heard nothing.

F ran out of the building and leapt into a taxi.

"Dahab. Now!"

In a second he was hurtling back through the desert towards the coast. Once there, F grabbed his gear from the hotel and high-tailed it to the taxi station for Taba.

Once he was safely across the border, he walked into a bar in Eilat and drank a beer. There were lots of other backpackers in the bar, Brits mostly, who had made their way back to Israel to renew their Sinai visas. A few, like F, were waiting for the bus to Tel Aviv.

The Brits were all deeply tanned and spent a lot of their time talking about their tans and complimenting each other on their tans and voicing their collective concern at how quickly their tans would fade once they returned to England. And F, being from Australia, just laughed and said to them, "Only mad-dogs and Englishmen go out in the midday sun. You silly bastards are all going to die of skin cancer."

When the bus departed, darkness had already fallen across the heat-hammered Negev.

F fell asleep but was woken up by the desperate pleas of one of the Brits.

"My boyfriend! My boyfriend! Help. He has passed out!"

F looked up and sure enough a man had slumped down, unconscious. F leapt to his feet in a somnambulant daze and charged down through the dark towards the driver. He stumbled hap-hazardly over Israeli soldiers that were sleeping on the aisle floor.

They cursed him in vitriolic Hebrew.

The driver remained unmoved.

"Look where we are? What do you expect me to do? We are in a desert!"

The driver had a point. Besides, what was one light-headed Gentile to a Jew who had been through a life of wars and strife?

F returned to his seat, more carefully this time, now uncomfortably aware of how many guns he had trodden on during his run down the aisle. The soldiers cursed him again as he passed by.

When he got to his seat, the Brit had recovered. F fell asleep, feeling embarrassed and stupid.

The new hotels of Tel Aviv shone and glistened where they hugged the corniche and the ocean.

But the fancy hotels were not for F. He had very little money and the most suitable accommodation, of the free variety, was to be found sleeping on the beach with the other penniless backpackers.

It was illegal to sleep on the beach and the police would force the backpackers to move on, as you would move a herd of cattle.

When they would settle for the evening, they slept in a circle, the men on the outside and the women on the inside, to prevent perverts and rapists from getting at the girls.

Nonetheless, hardly a night passed by without the screams of a girl being leapt upon by a psychopath, the nearest men getting up to enthusiastically beat the living crap out of the assailant.

There was no escaping the heavy awareness of danger and violence that permeated the scene. To F, it even seemed as if there was a seething undercurrent of tension and threat of conflict that was indigenous to the land itself, even there on the very edge of the shore, as if tainting the ocean, the waves retreating not merely from natural motion but also in distaste.

Not all of the members of the roving group were simple backpackers short of a buck. Many were straight out thugs and criminals who were hiding on the beaches to avoid the law. They had overstayed their visas and had nowhere to go. The migratory herd of flotsam that had been flung together was half-populated by vagabonds and desperados.

For these men, there was nothing noble about the ocean which lapped at their feet. Rather, it was only an obstacle and barrier to their escape.

One of the men was a South African, a Boer, blonde and handsome.

Beautiful Israeli girls would come down at night and sit on the Boer's lap and caress him with tender kisses. His errant comrades who were in on the story would sit around and leer and laugh, because the Israeli girls were under the shameful illusion that the Boer was actually a refugee who had fled the terrors of Bosnia and had no-one and no-where to go.

But the Boer, for all his boyish good looks, was the most vicious one of the whole lot.

One night F awoke to find the Boer beating up the man beside him. The Boer had his knee on the man's throat, laughing all the while. F didn't know what had caused the dispute, but the victim spent the rest of the night gasping for breath through his ruptured wind-pipe.

And it was the Boer and his accomplices who had noted that F actually did have at least a little money hidden away. Bad men have eyes like hawks.

So one night they got a bit of a party going and invited F into the fold. They passed him a bottle to drink, and that was about all that F could remember.

In the morning, when he came to, the Boer and his mates were gone.

So too were all F's belongings, his pack, passport, money, even his boots. He lay on the sand in his one pair of shorts and shirt and realized that everything else was gone.

Then he groaned and crawled into the waves and tumbled about in the surf, completely numb.

At the Australian Consulate he was given some strange looks. He was disheveled and had wandered all day through the streets of Tel Aviv, bare-feet burning on the pavement, with nothing to eat or drink.

"You're a bloody idiot son!" scolded the consul. "What the hell are you doing sleeping on a beach anyway?"

The consul was sitting behind a desk in an air-conditioned office.

He was ruddy and thick-set. Framed photos of rugby teams lined his desk, typical of a foreign office type, all beer and football.

He continued with more curses at F.

"Well here's the phone you bloody idiot. You better get some money wired over from somewhere, because you're going to need it to pay for the new passport."

On his way out a good-looking girl with shoulder-length red-hair was sitting behind a desk. She gave F a quizzical look.

"You don't even have shoes!" she exclaimed.

Something wild flared up within F. He felt an instant arousal. He may not have shoes but it was obvious to all how healthy and lean he was. He imagined in a flash her cool and luxurious apartment, she, offering him the couch to sleep on, but all in the name of further study, further observation, with the further aim, in F's mind, of untamed sexual abandon. He envisioned himself taking her and she being completely overwhelmed, that moment forever etched in her memories.

"You can borrow some of my boyfriend's shoes," she said.

"Ah shit!" said F, and simply turned away and walked off.

He was in no frame of mind to *work*. He had had about enough of everything. And, for whatever reason, he had no idea why, he made his way to Jerusalem and found the dirty hostel in the Arab Quarter. It was there he met Peer who listened to his tales.

Peer and F were on the roof of the hostel, drinking vodka.

F lay back and lit a cigarette. He had a strangely liberating, new-found, contented ease. He didn't know what it was, but it had come with all the adventures and trials and experiences. He had reached a point where he suddenly felt a lot older, but also felt as if nothing could kill him now, and how he was ready for anything.

"So tell me," asked Peer. "What was it like on top of Mount Sinai?"

F thought back through his recent experiences. He reflected on his night on the summit of the holiest of mountains. He recalled the filth and feces and the army of mindless tourists and the robotic inanity of clicking cameras.

"Ah, Mount Sinai," F said. "It is a very religious place."

CHAPTER TWELVE

The Old Man and the Turtle
Have a Discussion

The old man awoke with a start. He had the distinct sense of being watched.

His eyes gradually adjusted to the late afternoon light and, as his sight sharpened, he noticed an indistinct shape immediately before him on the grass.

"Greetings old man," said the turtle.

"I am old and my eyes are poor," said the old man. "But my ears are open. I sense in your tone the words of the slow-moving sleep-walker. Appropriate too, for I also have one foot in my dreams."

"What were you dreaming of old man?"

"A beautiful girl and a love that was lost."

"A love lost? How did you lose this love?"

"Through the folly of man."

"Through a folly of your own making?"

"No, through the folly of other men, of men who would forfeit this life for another."

"I detect remorse in your words, old man. Was your dream one of love or tragedy?"

"Ah turtle. Your wrinkles and ponderous tread bespeak wisdom. But your judgment is not sound! My dream was one of anger!"

"Anger?" said the turtle. "You humans are beyond comprehension. Am I not the most fortunate of beings, for I feel neither love nor anger?"

"You are fortunate indeed, but not as fortunate as I."

"How could man be more fortunate than the sleepy, sun-basking turtle, free of emotional torments? What is man but a pin-cushion of afflictions? A target shot to pieces by arrows? With a brain like a stirred-up ant's nest? An over-ripe melon crawling with flies? Man!" laughed the turtle. "Most wretched of beings! Man is nothing but a plethora of trials and travails."

"Turtle," said the old man. "You are famous for your deep thoughts. You move slowly and think deeply. You know the art of observation and reach profound conclusions. But when you crawl into your shell to sleep and contemplate how sapient and fortunate you are, tell me, what do you dream of?"

"Why?" said the turtle, bemused. "I cannot recall."

The old man laughed.

"Wise turtle, if I can tell you of your own lost dreams, does that make me wiser than you?"

"Go ahead," laughed the turtle. "Tell me my own dreams."

"Certainly," said the old man. "You dreamt of nothing. That is why you have nothing to remember."

"But is it not better to dream of nothing than to have dreams wrought by afflictions?" asked the turtle. "Do you not wake up tired from such dreams, wishing instead for oblivion in your sleep?"

"No, little turtle, and I will tell you why. Some say that men dream of their *afflictions*. That they dream of lusts and desires and anger and passion and sadness and much more besides. But here has your wisdom abandoned you. For these *afflictions* are not afflictions at all. Rather, they are *gifts*. They are gifts that are the very essence of man himself. These gifts make man rich and complex and able to dream. These gifts make man the most fortunate of creatures."

"Can man be both wretched and fortunate?" said the turtle.

"Man is indeed fortunate. But his gifts are unruly children. He tries to ride his gifts like one rides a wild bull. Man gets thrown down again and again. He gets discouraged and invents idols to give him comfort. Truly, only the greatest men can ride the wildest beasts."

"Old man, here my wisdom eludes me. I begin to wonder if you are not delusional. Perhaps age has made you senile?

"For how can a dream of anger be a gift? Do not men chastise themselves for their anger? Do they not castigate themselves for it? Do they not flagellate themselves because of it? Do they not attempt to purge themselves of it? Indeed, do they not pray for redemption because of it?"

"All that you say is true," said the old man. "But such men are liars and cowards. Such men are cast down from the wild bull. Indeed, these very men *would* pity such men!

"For if these men were honest, they would embrace anger as their brother and sadness as their sister, for such traits are integral to man, are born of man, and should be recognized as such. But where today is such a man to be found? Where is there a man who celebrates man? Where is there a man who does not want to be tamed and caged, but instead aches to ride the crest of a surging and crashing wave?"

"Can there really be such a man?" asked the turtle.

"Surely, wise turtle, I am this greatest of men."

CHAPTER THIRTEEN

The Old Man is Paid a Visit by the Priest

"Is that him out there, nurse?"

"Yes Father, down at the bottom of the garden, beneath the old oak tree."

The priest adjusted his dog-collar and wiped the sweat off his brow with a handkerchief.

"Is it sensible for him to be outside in such blistering heat?"

"The heat doesn't seem to trouble him Father. He is most content when he is outside. If he is shut inside for too long then he becomes quite frantic, almost as if he is in a rage."

The priest took another sip of tea and stared curiously out of the window at the stoic back of the old man.

"But I am confused. You said that he has never spoken?"

"Well, yes, that is true Father," said the nurse. "He is completely incapacitated. He can only move his eyes. But his eyes possess such a powerful expression that it is almost as if you can hear what he is saying. One gets to know these things after so long."

"Oh, I see," said the priest, placing his empty cup on the saucer.

"But there is no explanation for his condition? Are you certain there was no stroke?"

"That's correct Father. That is why they sent him here. For eleven years he has sat beneath the old oak tree and has not moved of his own volition or uttered a single word."

"Yes, yes," murmured the priest, impatiently.

The priest was not looking forward to leaving the cool of the building for the searing summer heat. His black frock was incompatible with that sort of weather.

"Well, I'd best get out there and pray for him. So, you don't even know if he is a Catholic?"

"No Father, like I said before, he arrived here in Virginia without any trace. No one knows a thing about him. It is a mystery."

The priest rose from the table and stepped towards the door. The nurse abruptly leapt to her feet, knocking the chair clumsily backwards.

"Father," she said. "I don't mean to be presumptuous but I suggest that you don't approach him. I would let that one go."

The priest stopped.

"Why?"

"Well, like I said, after so many years you get to know things. I get the strong impression that he might not be happy to see you."

The priest grew red in the face and shot the nurse a look of contempt.

"No one, I repeat, no one, is undeserving of the sublime love of God! I shall go now and pray so that this man may be absolved of his sins!"

And without further ado, but with an air of haughty disdain, the priest stepped out of the kitchen and into the garden.

The sun hit him with full force, physically jarring him, pressing down on him. It was midday and all was brilliantly illuminated with a fearful glare.

The priest's sandals and the hem of his frock made a crunching sound as he trod through the tinder-dry grass.

He walked around the oak tree and stood squarely in front of the old man. The sun was almost directly overhead, and there was no shade, spare the sliver that fell upon the old man. The priest was forced to stand in the full luminosity of the sun, and the sweat ran in steady rivulets down his face and neck.

"My son. Blessings be upon you."

The old man awoke and fixed his eyes upon the image in black before him.

"What is this dark figure? Could this be a devil? A demon? An ominous harbinger of sinister signs? Could this be the reaper himself? What? Is my time up? But wait! There is a familiar smell. A rotten smell. The stench of lies and deceit! Behold, the priest!"

"My son," said the priest. "I have been told you are mute but that you may still comprehend. I have come to pray for you, to pray that Our Father may loosen your tongue and heal you. With him, all things are possible."

"Priest! The tongue of my mind is loose and is ready to give you a lashing. Begone you ninny. You are disturbing my peace with your nonsense."

The priest leant down so that he could see the old man's face beneath the brim of his hat. The old man met his stare.

"My son I sense disquiet in you."

"At least one of your senses is working correctly," hissed the old man. "A shame indeed that your other senses have abandoned you, for you have eyes to see but are blind and ears to hear but are deaf. I know you well, you charlatan, and I know your type. You preach sin and death. You shun this world in favor of another. You see man as scum. You nefarious traitor! You toxic snake!

"Go and preach your lies elsewhere to some other fool, but do not impose upon me. Better yet, follow your own preaching and leave this world, abandon this greatest gift for the other world of your wretched imagination. You dishonor this life. Thus you dishonor my love. So Begone!"

"My son," said the priest. "Although you cannot speak I can sense your anger. You need redemption. I will absolve you of your sins. I will now pray for you."

The old man leapt within himself.

"You? Pray for me? I can barely conceive of such a blasphemy. It is I who should pray for you!

"And I would do so if I felt pity, but I only feel aversion and repugnance. I will honor my displeasure for I honor truth. And my displeasure trumpets loudly of your conceited ignorance.

"So go! Leave me now. Leave me with my love and take your wretchedness elsewhere. Do not offend my love with your piteous utterances."

The priest felt strangely uncomfortable but proceeded to fortify himself through his familiar actions.

"Let us pray. In the name of the Father, the Son, the Holy Ghost…"

"Don't do that! Don't you dare!" barked the old man. "Has the heat given you a soft head? Don't you dare speak of my love with such infamy."

"Redemption from your sins…"

"Redemption? Sins? Away blasphemer! Go eat your flesh and drink your blood!"

The priest reached out his hand and placed it on the old man's shoulder.

"Do not be afraid my son…"

Suddenly, the priest leapt backwards, recoiling in pain.

At first he thought he had received an electric shock. He cried out and grabbed his hand. Then, as he threw his head back in agony, the sun caught him clear in the eyes, blinding him, sending him into a swoon.

"Christ! Christ," he blustered, groping about in sightless whiteness, until the nurse appeared, and guided him back to the house, amidst much confusion.

CHAPTER FOURTEEN

The Old Man and the Wasp Speak of Religion

The old man laughed heartily.

"Ah wasp! Thank you! A most timely intervention!"

The wasp landed again on the left shoulder of the old man.

"Old man, I too enjoy a good joke, especially at the expense of another. After all, am I not a wasp?

"And how could I resist such a soft hand? One unblemished by the scars of labor? And the hand of a virgin to boot!"

"Indeed," said the old man. "The audacity to claim knowledge of life yet to know nothing of sex is the very height of absurdity! But forgive me little wasp, am I wrong in thinking you acted from kindness?"

"Old man, I like to stab, for that is my nature. That has worked out well for you. I like this stinging business, you know!

"But in saving you through my own joyous fury you remain in my debt. I demand another tale for your last one seemed unfinished, something was amiss."

"Discerning wasp! For my tale was but a prelude to a trial. Our hero has but approached the mountain of thorns that he must climb. But at least he now knows that it must be climbed!

"And at least he is now equipped for this undertaking, for now he knows something of love and movement, of art and honesty."

"Love! You are a fine one to speak of love old man. Do you think I didn't observe you with that priest? Where was your great love then?

Instead, I saw you spit venom like a snake. You cursed and condemned with the agitated fury of my own kind."

"Wasp, I still have my love. But I also have great anger if truth is violated. My anger leads to action in defense of noble truth. To not have anger would be to dishonor my love."

"But who is to know of the meaning of truth?" replied the wasp. "For this is but an arbitrary term holding different meanings for all beings."

"Wasp! A philosopher! Truly are we stunted by our grammatical limitations. Our miscommunications render us mute. But I can tell you this, the priest was an abomination of truth."

"Hence you honor your anger?"

"To not honor my anger at such blasphemy would be unpardonable. There is a time for love and a time for anger."

"But do not most men rebuke anger? Do not all men now follow the priest?"

"Yes, from humanity emanates a gangrenous odor."

"But where is their anger?"

"They have forsaken it."

"Why?"

"Men have become as meek as sheep and as docile as cattle put out to pasture. Men are no longer lions and bears. They have lost their distinguished strengths. They have lost their self-worth and dignity.

"Instead, men have been attacked by a cancer, a terrible cancer that has mutated them from the great and the wild into the weak and the tamed. Their thoughts have been fogged by weighty lies."

"What are these lies?" asked the wasp.

"These lies are the words of priests that condemn the very earth beneath us. Their words damn the earth as soiled and they curse man as impure. They look upon themselves with shame, and invent fallacies about a different life in a place of their imagination, so ashamed are they of this earth, my love.

"Thus my love grieves, for she has spawned hateful and ungrateful children. I tremble at her mournful laments!"

"Surely, this is a cancer indeed!" exclaimed the wasp.

"And who would not rage against a cancer with anger?" said the old man. "And I also swear this to you, wasp, I hold the same menace for the other preachers of death."

"Old man, first you spoke of love. But now you claim to know something of anger! Is this where your arduous search has brought you? Is anger the sour fruit born of your movement?"

"No. My anger is spurred by religion, that most formidable obstacle on the path to truth. To move artfully, to embrace honesty, without confronting religion, is impossible."

"Then speak to me old man," said the wasp. "Tell me a story of this religion, of that which drives you to anger.

"Tell of your ascent up the holy mountain of thorns!"

CHAPTER FIFTEEN

The Fifth Story

As F emerged from the water, he didn't see any angels or any shining light. No dove of peace descended from heaven. Yet, the crowd were on their feet, applauding. Some held their hands aloft. Many were singing.

"We expect great things from this young man," announced the minister to the congregation. "We will follow his future with great anticipation."

The minister had good reason to do so. F had given a very powerful speech. F was a very good speaker, and the crowd had risen to the occasion, as crowds are prone to do, especially when they hear what they want to hear.

Later, F walked through a throng of well-wishers who shook his hand in hearty congratulation.

F stepped outside onto the wet, cobbled streets of Oxford.

He departed immediately, striding at pace, heading in no particular direction. F glanced up at the gargoyles adorning the college facades. Water streamed off the revered roofs and out through the demonic mouths. It was almost night and the rain was steady.

F went into a pub and ordered a pint, not what most recently baptized people do, this is true, but F was not your average recently baptized person.

F stared steadily into the beer. A terrible and dark feeling consumed him. He wrestled with the meaning of it.

What was it?

What was this thing he had just done? Did he feel shame?

Yes! That was it. Shame.

But what was the nature of this shame?

Was it shame that he was going to get drunk by himself after getting baptized? Was it shame that he already knew that he would never be able to live according to a doctrine he had just moments before publically professed? Was it the shame for the disappointment soon to be emanating from the mouths of the flock as he 'strays'? That someone with so much promise should prove to be merely a seed thrown onto rocky ground, destined to wither away?

No. His shame was none of these things.

He drank heavily and looked ahead at his reflection in the pub mirror. And this is what he said to himself,

"I am ashamed at having been baptized. I am ashamed for being dishonest with myself. I am ashamed for being led astray by false teachings. I am ashamed for thinking I am sinful. I am ashamed for thinking I require redemption. I am ashamed for thinking so poorly of life that I would profess such absurdities."

And later, out on the road, in the sodden fog of the English night, he sank to one knee and cried this drunken lament,

"Forgive me, my love. I turn my face in shame at my words and actions. For I have maligned you and called you unworthy. And I have sold you in public before a rabble that bay for your blood. I have turned away from your embrace and slept with a deceitful whore. Forgive me these actions, my love."

And as F arose he felt enraptured, for he then knew that he didn't need forgiveness.

For life gave of herself willingly.

And was it not ironic that at the very moment when he thought he was handing over this life for another, the very opposite thing had happened? At the very moment that he had forsaken life he had seen that,

Life was precisely the thing that should never be forsaken.

He had taken himself to the heights of insanity in order to break through, so that all became clear.

From then on he could only ever consider religion as a sort of curio that you might find in an antique store.

But what interminable paths are followed to reach that perspective. So few have the stomach to travel on such vertiginous roads! Indeed, most never do. Yet the hypocrites argue that it is *they* that take the narrow and difficult paths. What perversion of mind is this? For surely the life of willful blindness follows the wide and easy road. Indeed, the blind man can only travel on a wide and open way!

Alas, poor humanity of such malleable mind, unarmored against the vast assault of pernicious doctrines. What chance does a being, born into the indoctrination of those sinister shackles, have of breaking *free*?

What chance of breaking free of synagogues and churches and mosques? What chance does a wee babe have, when reared on a mother's milk of the triple-breasted whore of Babylon? A rank and foul milk! Putrefied! Green like absinthe. And with a similar effect, eating into the brain like a worm.

What chance indeed!

And what children has this monstrous whore spawned? Does the trinity *really* defy logic? For I spy three bastard children all related. The elder is the bully and tyrant, arrogant and inbred, cross-eyed and unforgiving. Second is the cowardly, middle sibling, soft and weak and slippery. The youngest child is ambitious and malicious, yet as blind as a bat. These bastard brothers fight for preeminence. There can only be one! Their wars are constant. A constant affliction! Yet they all preach the same doctrine, 'Death to this Life!'

But wait! This story has begun at the end and is spiraling into the abyss. For now we need to return to the period of great innocence.

The Dawn Service, back in the church in the valley.

Grandfather is wearing his service uniform. Australian 9th Division, 20th Brigade, Infantry, medals testifying proudly of Tobruk and Alamein and Changi and Kokoda. Grandfather's hair is now a steel-grey beneath his slouch hat, but his back is ram-rod to attention, his thoughts still pounding with the booming guns of those events of long go, thumping explosions in the sand, his heart bursting with the screams of the twisted and gutted fallen.

The crowd stands silently before the minister. Then,

"They fell with their faces to the foe,
"They shall grow not old, as we that are left grow old,
"Age shall not weary them, nor the years condemn,
"At the going down of the sun and in the morning,
"We will remember them."

And the crowd in one solemn voice,

"We will remember them."

F is entranced, still half-asleep, as if in a dream of an old and sacred rite.

He imagines the battles and the dead. He trembles at the randomness involved, at the span of life determined by a step to the right or to the left. Which would it be? One unlucky bullet and all that has happened and gone before would be instantly no more. Every laugh and smile and tear and cry, every word and thought simply snuffed out and gone!

F glances around at the men in their uniforms, the lucky ones. How easily it could have been them. And even grandfather, F glances up at him, bronzed and strong, seemingly indestructible, how easily it could have been him. And if that had happened, F realizes with no small degree of shock,

"I would never have come to be."

F studies those around him out of the corner of his eye. He doesn't want to be caught staring.

But how he would love to gape!

It bewilders him so. Each person with a life all their own, each person waking, eating, working, thinking their own thoughts, each with their own lives and each life so different, each life so detailed and complex on a journey of its own.

And there are so many of them, these lives.

F considers *his* life, all of the things he sees, the bush and the valley and the land, all so rich and minutely painted.

Because it is all him!

It is his life and there is so much to it. His thoughts are his own and race through his head like wild horses. And he looks at the people and thinks of all of their own thoughts racing through their own heads, completely unrelated to and oblivious to his own thoughts.

Did they also look at other people and think the same things? Did they become overwhelmed with the sheer magnitude and heady abundance of the thought of life all around them? And not only at that point in time but in all times passed and in all times to come? Did they think of that too?

Of the infinite?

F is again relieved to return to the top end of the valley.

He leaps out of the car and bolts off into the bush like a stray cat.

That night he wanders alone in the moonlight. He climbs up the mountain behind the house and crouches on the edge of a sandstone ledge, high up.

F peers across the valley, shrouded in mist that rises mysteriously up from the riverbed and spreads out over the valley floor. There is not a human sight nor sound. Just the night sounds of the bush.

F is in his element.

But…

His mind is still traversing expansive and foreign terrains. He is thinking about life, *his* life. His mind is now compromised and baffled. There is a stripping of innocence. A rape is taking place. He is sensing his own mortality. Realizing, really realizing, for the first time, that he too will live and die.

And what of these words of the minister?

Who is this man of spiritual authority who leads? Who is this God that he speaks of? Who is this strange and inaccessible God, inventor of heaven and hell? Who is this God who sends his own Son to be nailed to a cross to redeem mankind? Why does the boy feel a repugnance and aversion to this God? Why does F feel suffocated in a church?

In a church he cannot *breathe.*

F gazes up at the firmament and prays,

"Oh God. They say that faith can move mountains. But they also say that You are not to be tested. I am by myself here before You. Surely You could make me fly?"

F stands up. His bare feet are planted on the sandstone.

"Oh God. There is no one else here and I speak to You with honesty. Just grant me this one thing, oh all-powerful God. Just hold me aloft when I jump off this stone. You control all things great God. You can heal the sick and raise men from the dead. You are the grand creator, the master of life. You can lift me up by the merest command.

"God, just grant me this one thing, and I will believe in You and worship You forever, for I will know that You are true."

F surveys the heavens. He contemplates all that he sees. He considers the depths of space. He equates all sensations with thoughts of this God and fills his chest with air and raises his arms up high with his palms to the sky and imagines, no, actually *feels* that God is coursing through him from his head to his toes, that he and God are a coalesced whole.

Then he leaps up! To rise ever upwards! Up into the empyreal radiance of God!

But he immediately returns to earth.

F remains crouched on the edge of the ledge for a long time. The night is growing cold. He blends into his surrounds, perching like a cast effigy, as still as an eagle, patient, a simulacrum inseparable from his surrounds, drawn by gravity to the ground, to the stone, to the bush.

There he stays.

F prides himself in knowing the land.

Perhaps pride is not the correct term?

Better to say he gains *great pleasure* from knowing the land.

From knowing not only what lies behind every rock and tree, but how to climb each mountain, where the secret passages are that lead up through the rocks, which bends of the river hold the deepest water, where to spy for eels, which trees to avoid in the orchards for fear of wasps, or how to spot the bull-ants and soldier-ants, or where the red-backed spiders hide beneath the melons, or what is being grown in every field in the valley, and how the freshly turned earth feels beneath his feet and between his toes, and how all these things *smell*.

And F loves to listen to the old farmers talk over their beers after work, with their leathery skins and gnarly hands and feet, made even darker by the earth, of the crops and the rain and the heat, and the price of cattle and corn, and the snakes they saw, and best of all, of the old times.

Of tales of floods and fires, of names now ground to dust but still remembered in myth and fable, of the early days when white men first came up the river and settled and broke the land.

Of Phipps, the first man to run a ferry upriver, and the convicts brought up on the ferry to cut the track through the wilds to the hinterlands, and how they first ran the cattle through the bush on the track and got them into town by ferry, making Phipps rich, at least rich according to the standards of those times.

And they would talk about how Phipps had built a shack by the ferry-landing, which served as both tavern and brothel for the drovers after they had run the cattle through the bush.

Phipps brought the girls up from Sydney on his boat, just as he brought up the convicts in their chains, under armed red-coat guard, a world away from their homes, destined never to return, knowing full well they never would, to live bare-foot and swinging picks and axes at rock and tree, carving deeper and deeper into the bush, where many of them would perish because of hunger or snakebite or just from the sense of madness that comes with being thrown into the farthest desolation beyond any reasonable comprehension.

And the old farmers would sip on their beers and silently reflect on those convicts and how it all was back then, and they would talk about the convict tombstones they had found years ago by Phipps's landing, carved on rough-hewn slabs by illiterates, the strangest tombstones ever seen, with the words 'Gone To God' carved over and over again and in every direction, giving the epitaph more the appearance of a Ouija board or pentagram or some such other devilish insignia.

And then they would talk about how there was nothing left of Phipps's shack because flood after flood had swept it all away and nothing was ever built of any permanence of structure because everyone was so poor and existence was simply that, existence, a matter of survival, and how it took men like Phipps to take on the bush and survive, strong men who could carry three sacks of potatoes at a time, one on each shoulder and one across the back. And strong in spirit too, though not necessarily good in spirit, for Phipps was known to be brutal and treated everyone else like a dog, for how else was he going to make things run with convicts and whores and rum-drunk soldiers and drovers all primed to brawl.

For that was how it was in the old times.

F loved to listen to the stories, and then he would be out looking around, searching around the tidal limits of the river for evidence of Phipps' shack, walking the old tracks to the hinterland and studying the convict built roads, some in gullies with layers of hand-cut rock stacked forty feet high, and looking for old tombstones or any evidence of those old days.

Or the days that were even older, the days before the white man.

The old farmers didn't talk about those days so much, about the aboriginal times. The farmers knew where the tribal places were and where to find the cave-paintings, but those secrets were rarely surrendered.

There were some things considered best not spoken of and the aboriginal days were veiled and perplexing to the white man.

Perhaps it was because, like F, the old farmers also *felt* it.

For they too had once been boys and they too had wandered the land and knew the land as F did. And they too could sense that there was more to the land than could be simply seen or smelt or tasted. There was something old in the land, something hoary and dormant, something of the earlier men.

F heard every word, as boys do, and he learnt, from a drunken slip here and there, where the various *places* were, the sacred places in the caves with the paintings, the grooves in the rocks near the lagoons where the aborigines would sharpen their spears and hunt kangaroos as they came down to drink. And it was known that there were certain places where strange events were witnessed, of *min-min* lights in the distant trees. And there were also places where women would not go on account of feeling a lead-lined cloak of unease descend and enshroud them, the places of male initiation where the aborigines had run wild in hallucinatory horror after eating daytura plants.

F took great pleasure in knowing all of these things.

When Old Ed Mason let slip about the cave, F had no sooner heard than he was scrambling through the bush and on his way.

Old Ed Mason felt a twinge of regret as he watched F go.

But it was too late by then, for the words had been spoken and he knew the boy *had* to go.

The moon was full and the valley opened up before him, bathed in a shimmering glow. As F ran through the brush down towards the river the words repeated themselves over and over in his thoughts.

"The tribe was moving down the valley.
"It was the last walkabout.
"An old woman was dying on a sand-bank.
"They carried her up to the cave and rocked her in.
"Then they left."

F was beyond the top end now and in the true wilderness. The mountains had closed in and the river-banks were impassable, so F followed the path of the river itself. At the darkest hour, F reached the crossing-point.

When he emerged from the river F stopped to drink and thought he saw something of unusual shape in the mist by the far bank. But when he took a second glance, he only saw the mist.
So he went on, clawing his way up the bank, and once over the crest it was just like Old Ed Mason had said, opening up around a lagoon, cradled by the mountains beyond.

"You couldn't get a better location.
"Loaded with fish and wallabies and kangaroos and goannas and
snakes.
"Best aspect for it.
"Plenty of grub.
"But make no mistake boy, that gully is steep and slippery.
Rainforest."

F made his way across to the lagoon and entered the thick foliage of
rainforest and looked carefully around. He began to ascend the gully,
climbing up into the rocks.

Ahead of him was a prominent cliff, and at the base of the cliff was
the cave. With a growing sense of discomfort he approached the
cave-entrance.

There, he halted and waited for his eyes to adjust.

F climbed inside and felt the velvety soft accumulation of eons of
sand beneath his feet. He was very weary and sat down in the sand
and then lay down to catch his breath. Then before he could think of
anything he was asleep.

How long he had been asleep he could not tell.

Maybe he hadn't actually fallen asleep at all. Maybe he was in that
state in-between the knowing and unknowing?

But either in dream or wakefulness he discerned the breathing sound,
at first bordering on the imperceptible, like the sound of an engine
from far away, edging in and out of hearing. But then it was
unmistakable and F's heart beat faster inside his chest and he froze
in fear. And the breathing matched his own heart-beat and grew
louder until it filled the cave and boomed in his head and still he
could not move and he clenched his whole body and screwed his
eyes up tight.
And F knew that the breathing was that of an old voice, the voice of
a woman, gasping and gulping for air.

Then he was plunging and tumbling back down the gully, plunging and tumbling through the vines and scrub, emerging breathless and bloodied at the tree line, and then sprinting back to the river where he collapsed, and let the current carry him downstream.

"Find it?" asked Old Ed Mason, rocking back on the porch.

"I reckon I did."

They sat in silence.

Then after a while F said, "I don't reckon I'll ever go back there again."

"Someone had to know," said Old Ed Mason.

They sat and peered into the bowels of the bush, away across the valley.

And the bush stared right back at them.

CHAPTER SIXTEEN

The Old Man Discovers His
Relation to a Snake

A blaze of burnished gold hung in the western sky and the shadows grew long.

Dusk.

Soon, a copperhead emerged from beneath a rock, not far from the old man, and lay flat on the rock surface, absorbing the radiant heat.

The snake contemplated the old man, its tongue flicking in and out, as if speaking. And this is what the snake said, "I like you old man."

The old man stirred and spied the snake.

"Is it good to be liked by the most condemned of all creation?"

"Old man, I sense there is something of the snake in you too."

"How so?"

"I sense that you too are a loner and that you too are despised by men. I sense that other men would like to dash your skull beneath their heels. I have heard you speak and you carry venom in your words. And I have seen you torment this wasp."

"I did not intend to torment the wasp."

"But torment it you have. Your stories have driven the wasp into a fury, flying in circles before your sleeping eyes, not knowing whether or not to sting you."

"Why snake?" asked the old man. "I have simply tried to save my own skin! At my age, the sting of a wasp would spell the end for me.

Tormenting has had nothing to do with it. I would say I have done well, if I remain un-stung."

"Then why," asked the snake, "does the wasp fly in peevish circles?"

"Because the wasp is confused. The wasp expects a simple story, but has not yet grasped that there is no such thing. The simple truth is that all is connected. The wasp is yet to discover that it is impossible to speak of a single subject without considering the all."

The snake lay silently for a while, and then spoke again.

"I'm not so sure you are speaking truthfully, old man. I smell deceit. Again, I sense the snake in you."

"Surely snake there is something in what you say," conceded the old man. "For I am as old and wise as a snake and I can also spit venom. I am at once both beautiful and fearsome. I have many skins and regenerations. But I am not deceitful. Indeed, I am the embodiment of truth. And truthfully I tell you this, in a younger day I would not have hesitated to dash your skull beneath my heel."

"Well, why not now?" hissed the snake.

"I can no longer move," said the old man. "I am so old that my body is a shadow of my former self. But make no mistake, I still burn fiercely within."

"What say I bite you now old man, for you seem helpless to me?"

"That would be in keeping with your character."

"Old man, you toy dangerously with me. Do you not fear death?"

"Why should I fear death when it is as much a part of nature as birth? And I have lived a full and long life, which is more than many are granted."

"Would you consider your death by my bite a good death?"

"It would not be the best death."

"So there is a best death? Tell me, what is that?"

"In ancient times," said the old man, "there was only one best death, to die as a warrior, to risk one's existence as a combatant in the ultimate contest that embodied the height of human pathos. Therein was found glory.

"But in this age there is no glory in death. The men of this age want to grow old. Too old! They continue to live although their faculties are already dead. They dribble and mumble and stare at walls. They soil themselves and need to be cleaned. Oh most horrendous humiliation! This is what the man of today aspires to. Longevity has taken the place of glory, but at what cost?"

"But old man, you have missed your chance to die such a death!"

"Yes snake, I too have grown old. But also, there are no longer any warriors. There are only cowards who fling their stones from afar."

"So what is there for you old man? Can you have a good death?"

"Yes. A good death is to die nobly and triumphantly. To die with fear is to dishonor life. When death comes one should stand tall and show others how they should die."

"And thus you wait?"

"And thus I wait."

"Old man, there is something of you that is anachronistic. Maybe it would be best if you should die, for other humans are meek and mild, while you carry something of old within you."

"Snake, perhaps you are right. This world is not made for the likes of me. Man has grown poorly and is pale and wan like a sickly child. Man of today is a limp and pathetic creature, altruistic and egalitarian, all-forgiving and self-condemning.

"Yet I embrace the ancient nobility of man. I love all of life and all elements of life. That includes all things abhorred by the man of today, for I love hatred, conflict, combat, trials, fury, raging torrents of passion, the bursting of bombs, the striking of lightning bolts, and I even love death and embrace it as a brother."

"Surely old man, you are a conundrum. It is no wonder that the wasp flics in circles!"

"Dear snake," said the old man. "You spend most of your days lazing around and your mind has grown lazy. For I am no conundrum, but am man as man is intended to be.

"Monumental. Epochal!"

CHAPTER SEVENTEEN

The Wasp Teases the Old Man

Summer was at its zenith and the wasp darted about in heated frenzy.

"Old man. Awake! For I am in a violent passion and the sight of your constant dozing only agitates me all the more. How dare you sleep in pompous contentment while the sun verily crackles overhead! What is most irksome to me? The heat of high summer or your outrageous claims? Truly my venom boils in my tail!"

The old man awoke and gave a cheerful laugh.

"Greetings wasp! We meet again. I must say, you are in a right state aren't you? Has the heat gone to your head? In all truth you seem most distressed."

"Truth! Old man, your words slither like the snake. One moment they are to my right and in a flash they are to my left. Who can tell where the truth may lie?"

"Indeed wasp," agreed the old man. "The truth is both to your left and to your right, or wherever you may find my words."

"Hah!" scoffed the wasp. "You speak in circles just as I fly. Just listen to your stories. They start in one place yet finish in another. Is there no end to such madness? For just look at your last tale, I demanded talk of religion and you twisted it into a ghost story of goblins and ghouls?

"Tell me, old man, when I ask you to speak of up will you speak of down? Of left will you speak of right? Of north will you speak of south? And now you boast to the snake to also know something of death! Certainly, if I ask you to speak of death you will no doubt speak of life!"

"Wasp," the old man replied. "There is nothing confusing in my words. The words may appear to move, but see how you yourself fly in circles? Do my words move or do you? And besides, knowledge of death will come soon enough, and with it knowledge of life."

"Enough with your riddles you meddlesome old man! You have me so hot I should just sting you as things stand."

"How I love your passions, wasp! Summer is at its hottest and you are in the prime of your life. You are young and violent and ready for war, but one day you too will move more slowly and cease to fly in circles."

"Oho. Here it is again!" said the wasp. "The voice of wisdom from the aged sage. Silly old fool."

"Little wasp, I too was once young and passionate and have wielded an honest sword as surely as you wield an honest sting. And I tell you truly, honesty dictates a love of death."

"Old man, I know of one thing you have no knowledge of," teased the wasp.

"Oh?"

"Friendship! For how may a man who loves death have friends? There is no room for friendship in your diabolical formula. Is it any wonder that day after day you sit in this yard and no one comes to visit you?"

"Dear wasp, I can tell you this, friends are difficult to keep. Friends of youth become stale in spirit. As people age, they are more easily offended and then they are lost. They also grow old and die. Surely, I have lost more friends than I have had."

"There you go again with your preposterous claims!"

"Not so," countered the old man. "I have had many enemies who were friends lost to me before I even knew them. And most tragic of all were those lost to religion, for they are the living dead. Surely it is better to be a friend to ghosts and goblins than a friend to religion."

The wasp flew in fury before the face of the old man.

"Look at the sun overhead old man. See how that fireball can barely be contained? It whips the earth and would like nothing more than to set the whole ablaze. That is nothing compared to my anger. Take heed old man, you aggravate me no end."

"And what balm could soothe this aggravation?" asked the old man.

"Tell me a tale, old man. Explain how you found friendship, oh great lover of ghosts and death!"

CHAPTER EIGHTEEN

The Sixth Story

Egil had been drinking all afternoon and was in full lecturing mode,

"*Great men are above humanity.*

"Think of them. Alexander. Caesar. Genghiz. Napoleon. Hitler. Do you think these men became conquerors by caring about individuals? No! They knew that people had to die. It didn't matter if it was one or a million. Statistics were irrelevant. These were men of grand action."

Egil took a swig of beer and lit a cigarette. Though ostensibly having a conversation with F, he was really giving voice to an internal monologue.

"Just look at Alexander the Great. Good old A the G! Everyone views him as the heroic ideal, romantic, brave, tragic.

"But come on! He was a mass-murdering psychopath. He cared nothing for human life. He led his own men on a wild goose chase across Asia, and thousands of them died along the way. He even killed his childhood friend in a drunken rage. These days you'd be up for murder. But people wax lyrical about how magnificent Alexander was. Well, the only truly magnificent thing about Alexander is that he raised himself above the common human condition. Thousands of people died for him, but that allowed him to achieve his aim.

"The achievement of his aim is what made him great!"

F ordered another two beers. It was happy-hour and the drinking was in full swing. Outside it was a mild Sydney afternoon. The sky was clear and the smell of eucalyptus wafted in the windows from the gum-trees.

The drinkers were raising an ever-growing din, the Friday night crowd coming in to get tanked, sculling beers, smoking cigarettes, joking and yelling. The greyhounds were racing on the television and bets were being slapped down on the bar.

They had been in the pub all afternoon. The university was located just up the road, and the pub served as a sort of second office for their 'academic' discussions. They should have been busy preparing for the expedition. They left in a week.

But around noon, as usual, Egil had developed a thirst and the pub had beckoned.

"Come on," he said. "Just a few beers over lunch won't hurt."

As they headed down the road to the pub, they were both fully aware that once at the bar they would stay put until closing. Sure, they would discuss the upcoming archaeological expedition and the search for the origins of Zoroastrianism, but conversation would inevitably spiral off in other directions.

F wasn't overly concerned. With Egil, most things seemed to miraculously work out. F was by now familiar with the pattern, everything done at the last moment, but remarkably, no disasters.

Anyway, what was F, a mere postgraduate student, supposed to do? Egil was the Project Director and F's academic mentor, so if Egil said they had to go to the pub, then that meant they had to go to the pub.

Far be it from F to disobey an order!

Besides, F never felt like he was missing anything by not being on campus. An afternoon in the pub with Egil was an education in itself. With a few beers under his belt Egil would lead F down intellectual paths rarely traveled in the somewhat staid cloisters of the quadrangle.

Egil was now talking in an uninterrupted stream.

"Napoleon was the same. Just look at the Egyptian campaign. He simply abandoned his troops and left them to their doom. Their lives were only a means to an end. And Napoleon was only upset because he had failed to achieve his objective. He didn't give a toss about the men who lost their lives.

"And look at the Moscow campaign, same thing. Napoleon was pushed on by his vanity, by his desire to grasp his grand ideal. And when the situation turned sour thousands of Frenchmen froze to death, which," chuckled Egil, in his characteristically mischievous way, "wasn't necessarily such a *bad* thing. God knows I don't care much for the French! But the point here is that none of the dead are remembered, except for Napoleon. His actions made him great. He placed himself *above* the common lot of humanity."

F took a look at Egil. He stood out against the general backdrop of drinkers. Tall and lean with an angular Prussian head, he couldn't have been more different to the sloppy office workers around him, with their collared white shirts, loose ties, and bloated, sedentary bodies. Although in his fifties, Egil possessed a more youthful aspect, as someone of a more nomadic and resilient demeanor than the rest of the crowd.

A momentary lull in Egil's monologue allowed F to get in a question.

"Why does greatness always have to be equated with war and conquest? I mean, some would say that Jackson Pollock was great. Others would say that Mother Theresa was great."

Egil shot F a contemptuous look over the rim of his glass.

"Christ, haven't you learned anything? I'm not talking about painters and do-gooders here. No one is going to remember Jackson-bloody-Pollock or Mother-bloody-Theresa in a thousand years. I'm talking about people who changed the face of history on a large scale. Look at Alexander. His actions determined the course of world history in a dramatic fashion. The results of his actions were so significant that he *has* to be remembered. That's the sort of greatness I'm talking about. Greatness, like genius, is a term too often bandied about, all too readily applied to those undeserving of the title."

He glanced at F skeptically and grinned.

"I know you are at a university but at least *try* to think intelligently will you?"

F smiled. He recalled being in Jordan with Egil some years back, driving through the Hauran, when a flock of sheep had blocked the road.

"Look! Postgraduates!" Egil had said with a sardonic laugh, such was his view on the paucity of modern academic standards.

"Then what about Hitler?" F asked. "According to your reasoning he would also qualify as a great man?"

Egil ordered two more beers and took a long, thoughtful look at the dogs racing on the television.

"Hitler was no different from the others. The reason why people place Hitler in a different category is that he existed within living memory. But other men have also committed immeasurable atrocities. Stalin also did, but a lot of Russians today certainly consider Stalin to be great."

Egil turned on his stool.

"Look. People will put you up on the cross for saying this, but if you are going to call Alexander 'great', or Napoleon 'great', then you also have to call Hitler 'great'. He is already one of the most significant figures of history. His actions changed the course of world history on a huge scale. Just think of the ramifications. The War. The Holocaust. The State of Israel. Conflict in the Middle East between Muslims and Jews. And now, a global conflict between East and West.

"But the *real* point here is that Hitler achieved his place in history, his notoriety if you like, because he placed himself *above* the common lot of humanity. He lived only for his ideals. The measure of carnage he created was irrelevant to him, in comparison to the measure of his achievement. In that sense, he was great."

F looked out the window. It was getting dark outside and the air was chilly with the oncoming night. The pub was full now. Drunken patrons stumbled around, spilling beer about the place.

Egil was oblivious to it all. He was deep in thought. F threw him another question.

"Well, according to your reckoning there won't be another *great* man for a couple of hundred years. They don't seem to come along very often."

Egil snapped out of his trance and hit F on the arm, as if punishing him for his naiveté.

"No, no! Great men are among us *all* the time. Whether they fulfill their destiny is entirely dependent upon time and place.

"I too could have been great if the conditions were right. For I understand what it takes to place an ideal above simplistic human sentiment. But that was not my destiny. Alexander and Napoleon had a nation or a people to fight for. I have spent my life drifting around the world. I have no ties or allegiance. Who can I fight for? I have no one to conquer. I was not born for these times."

Egil ordered more beer, lit another cigarette and took a long drag.

F didn't want to let it go.

"So are you saying that human life means nothing to you? That you could sacrifice a life?"

Egil exhaled with a rush of smoke, indicating that the answer should have been self-evident.

"Of course I could. Hundreds. Thousands. Millions. It's of no consequence. I would be pursuing a grand ideal and I have the resolve to pursue it even if people must die. Besides, all people die. It's simply a question of when."

"So you would be willing to kill to achieve an ideal?"

Egil leveled his eyes at F.

"Yes. Why? You don't believe me? You think I don't know what it's like?"

F had moved to the edge of his seat in an effort to detect any hint of deceit in Egil's words. Egil's face remained cold and expressionless. He spoke in a heavy, measured tone, as if he wasn't to be pursued on the subject.

But F continued, "So how about all of these people in this pub then? Would you have any qualms about killing all of them to achieve your goal?"

Egil didn't flinch.

"None in the slightest."

F drew on his cigarette and asked the question that begged to be asked.

"Then how about me Egil? Would you kill me? Your trusty lieutenant?"

Egil stared at F with a stony gaze. The noise of the evening crowd had grown to a clamor around them.

"Yes," he said calmly. "If I had to."

Egil and F sat silently amidst the red faces, the breaking glasses, the coarse laughter and the drunken yells.

And then Egil laughed.

"But of course I would never have to. You're my trusty lieutenant!"

Egil hit F cheerfully on the arm. F sat back and eyed Egil doubtfully.

"Egil, you sure can talk some bullshit."

Then they got really drunk.

The plane was a Soviet antiquity, a tiny twin-prop that appeared to be held together with tape and glue.

An eternity passed before the plane left the ground and then rose, ever so slowly, and even then never seemed to achieve the proper cruising altitude. They flew disconcertingly close to the ground for the duration of the journey. F felt they would drop out of the sky at any moment.

Looking out of the window F could see the massive wastes of the Kizil-Kum Desert stretching off over the horizon. The late afternoon sun simmered threateningly, shrouding the impenetrable sand dunes with a smoldering redness that flowed like lava, a truly apocalyptic scene.

The seats were small, the air stuffy, and their clothes wet with sweat. Two days of travel had left them bleary and dirty, and there seemed nothing for it but to have a drink. Egil pulled out a bottle of bourbon and the stewardess brought plastic cups of warm soda.

F slumped into a state of grimy delirium. The sun gave a final flare and dropped below the horizon. As time passed F blinked out of the window at the veil of heat and darkness. After an indeterminate period he detected lights below, isolated in the black desert ocean of the night.

Nukus.

Disembarking, F tried to get his bearings. The air was hot and heavy and the heat of the day, still saturated in the tarmac, radiated up through his boots. The luggage was thrown out the back of the plane straight onto the runway.

F found his bags and started walking. The terminal itself was closed and cloaked in darkness. A few electric lights spluttered over a gate that bypassed the main building and led straight into town. The gate had been left open for late arrivals. There were no officials to check their papers.

Beneath the lights lurked the wiry, hunched figure of Nikolai.

Egil smiled and gave Nikolai a big hug.

"Nikolai my comrade, so good to see you."

Nikolai squirmed in annoyance and pushed Egil away.

"Egil, you are fool. Stop being fool," he puffed haughtily.

Egil laughed. The two men could not have appeared more different, Nikolai, thin, grimacing, beaten, bitter and envious; and Egil, confidant, tall, strong, with a clear, intelligent face, his character armored, seemingly indestructible, as if designed by some superior motive.

Egil sensed Nikolai's irritation and deliberately began to annoy him further by being effusively cheery. He placed a hand on Nikolai's shoulder and made a show of sniffing the air.

"Ah. Smell that? Paradise! But where are we? Paris? Bavaria? Arcadia? No, of course! We're in Nukus! Back in the U.S.S.R."

F thought Nikolai was going to blow his top. Egil was pushing all the right buttons. Those references to the U.S.S.R were sure to set him off. Nikolai flinched. How he longed to be back in the U.S.S.R! But now it was all gone. Broken up into little pieces. There was no longer any order or structure. Society was sick with corruption. Nothing worked. The water was undrinkable. The land was ruined by over-irrigation and salinization. Nothing grew. The Oxus River was now so heavily irrigated that it no longer even reached the Aral Sea, which, as a result, was evaporating.

It was all a terrible *catastroph*.

And what of Nikolai's much-loved hometown, Nukus? Once a gleaming example of Soviet town-planning and the capital of The Semi-Autonomous Republic of Karakalpakstan, but now a malfunctioning toxic dump in the middle of nowhere, a polluted and dangerous dive surrounded by desert for thousands of miles, a summer hell of blasts of sand that choked your throat and stung your eyes, rubbish everywhere, flies swarming over the filth.

F blinked out of the car window at the passing apartment blocks, invariably tumbling into ruin, and at the pipes for transmitting hot air, albeit intermittently, that ran parallel to the road, waist-high, clad in asbestos, now tattered and frayed.

Nikolai, being a Professor, had been given one of the more desirable apartments on the top floor. At least, that was how things had stood when the apartments were first built. But now, the lack of water pressure meant he had to descend six flights of stairs with a bucket to get water from outside, where, in the shadows, lurked an acrimonious and vodka-soaked people.

The next evening, Egil and F wandered across to the bar in the basement of the Hotel Tashkent.

The bar was a seedy dive by any standard. The lights were dim with dust. The walls were plastered with sweat and grime. Russian music played. Hookers sat in dark corners smoking cigarettes, bored expressions on their faces. Tough looking Tartars kept a killer's eye on the scene.

The sense of danger provided F with a certain rush. He had to be on his toes, watching his wallet, drinking, but remaining alert to any drunk that might swing around to confront him. F knew by the faces of the drinkers that there was no room for bullshit. No one engaged in posturing or smart-talk. If people argued then knives came out, iron-bars came out, and people got stabbed, beaten and killed. And no one would be any the wiser.

Egil and F sat at the bar, smoking cigarettes and ordering vodka with beer chasers. The vodka was served in sealed plastic cups. F had to peel the lid off the cup before having a drink, pretty high-class stuff.

Egil carried all of the dig-funds on his body, over sixty thousand American dollars in cash. If anyone at the bar had known...

The atmosphere of Nukus was charged. F loved the dark and seedy bars, the tough guys drinking vodka, the volatile characters, and the dense odor of danger that hung heavily in the air. He didn't want to be anywhere else on earth, for in that fog of violence and hopelessness, he could detect the powerful threads of tragic romance.

Nikolai refused to join them at the bar. He was clearly pained to see them. Their presence was almost too much to bear. The insult wasn't simply that he had to share *his* archaeological project, but that he also had to co-direct the project with Egil, instead of being the sole grand poobah as he was accustomed. This affront to his authority caused his chest to tighten with rage.

But Nikolai needed the money.

Funding for his department had almost completely evaporated and the excavation equipment was antiquated. Even simple items, such as string, were difficult to obtain. String was something Egil could provide. He could also bring money, and that made the shame of having to work with Egil just that little bit more palatable.

On the other hand, Nikolai was responsible for arranging the logistics and supplies. Nikolai, inwardly furious at having none of the financial control, became very secretive about the other arrangements. He would keep Egil and F in the dark as to how the preparations were progressing and would only communicate with them sporadically. Sometimes, they wouldn't hear from Nikolai for days at a time. He refused to tell them when they should expect to depart for site, keeping them in a constant state of limbo.

In the meantime, Egil and F stayed in a single room apartment that was completely devoid of ventilation. The room was as hot as an oven. Each morning they would head into the market before the heat of the day became intolerable. Iron stalls selling shoes, clothes, nails, food and an endless array of miscellaneous junk, flanked the alleys of the bazaar. In the bazaar a man sold bottles of beer that he tried to keep cool in a bucket of water. They would stand in the midst of the bustle, sip on the lukewarm, watery, yeast-laden beer, and watch the world go by.

During the evenings they would sit outside the apartment, trying to catch any faint wisp of a breeze. The door to the apartment faced out onto a dirt courtyard surrounded by concrete walls. A canopy of withering grapevines crawled over the doorway. The vines had been planted for the purpose of shade, but in the relentless sun had shriveled to a bare skeletal frame now thickly coated with the dust that blew in from the desert. A bench was placed beneath the canopy.

Egil and F would sit on the bench late into the night and tell stories. Honesty was never the aim of the exercise. Truth was irrelevant. Lies were welcome.

Egil did most of the talking. He spoke about helicopter drops in the Jordanian Desert, of working the mines in Canada, of sailing across the Atlantic, of studying archaeology in London, of shooting at Russians in Afghanistan.

To Nikolai, Egil would say, "Isn't life funny Nikolai? Twenty years ago I would have tried to shoot you. But now, we are working together. All in the name of archaeology.

"Perestroika! Perestroika!"

Egil would throw his head back and laugh. Nikolai would stare at the ground and frown.

The first time F met Egil was at a function in the archaeology museum at the university. Egil was dressed as if he had just come back from the desert, which, incidentally, he had. F was struck by the empty look on his face that betrayed a blank disregard for those around him. Egil headed straight for the wine and poured a pint glass of red before walking outside to smoke a cigarette.

"There he goes," someone had whispered to F, with a nod of the head. "The man himself."

"Watch out for Egil," F was told. "He's not to be trusted. He's unpredictable. A powder-keg. If you get him in a bad mood, he might just turn around and punch your head off your neck. A genius to be sure, but one to be avoided. Certainly don't work with him. Bad for your career. Damnation by association, you know."

It was true that many big-named professors were furious with Egil, as they were unused to having their egos publicly trampled at international conferences. Egil had made a lot of enemies.

But when F went outside for a cigarette, Egil was both congenial and the very embodiment of enthusiasm, delighted to be in his element, talking about his true love, archaeology.

And with Egil's words F was transported down the Oxus River, fresh from the ice melt off the Hindu Kush, past the crossing used by Alexander, down, down to Karakalpakstan, to the birthplace of Zoroaster, to the fire-temples, to the lands of the Massagetae, the killers of Cyrus the Great.

And a whole new world opened up for F, one of a romantic quest of great magnitude, where he could grasp for an elixir of knowledge, for a potion that would send him in pursuit of history with the grand goal of understanding mankind in its very essence.

Nikolai woke them early without any warning. The truck was waiting outside, fully loaded with tables, chairs, tents, shovels, buckets and other archaeological paraphernalia.

"Come on! Come on! It's time. We must get to site. We are late," he blurted out.

In a bleary haze, F stumbled about, trying to get his gear together. All the while Nikolai paced the floor impatiently, wringing his hands, saying, "Qvickly, qvickly."

The road south from Nukus sliced through a stark desert landscape. The truck rumbled on for hours through a barren world. From time to time they would catch a glimpse of the Oxus River, off to the west, birthing a sliver of green that leapt out against the endless expanse of sand. A sky of the palest blue arced above them. Thunderous blasts of hot air whipped their hair into their eyes and scorched their faces. The canvas roof of the truck beat deafeningly in the heat.

F felt discombobulated sitting in the back of the truck, perched upon piles of equipment. The passing horizon of golden sand dunes held a timeless aspect, rolling on forever. The landscape remained unchanged and F peered off into the distance, falling into hypnotic stupefaction.

Then, off a way, F detected a brick tower, some fifty feet high, standing alone, a sentinel in the boundless waste. He sat up straight to get a better view and squinted through the glare.

"Dakhma! Dakhma!"

He recalled one of Egil's impromptu pub lectures.

"To the cynical and clinical Western mind, the Zoroastrian faith is characterized by many strange practices. Among these are strict funerary rites, which include exhumation, or exposure of the corpse to the elements. Because the concept of purity is central to Zoroastrianism, there is no greater impurity, or pollutant, than death. The corpse has to be treated in a very specific manner.

"First, the body is laid out and bathed in bull urine, which functions as a powerful disinfectant. Three circles are drawn on the ground around the body, in order to keep the impurities of the corpse in a confined space. Zoroastrians believe that the spirit hovers around the body for three days, so the corpse is kept within this state for that period. At the end of the three days, a dog is brought in to gaze at the body, because the dog is thought to possess the special ability to distinguish between life and death. The gaze of the dog signifies that the time has come to move the body to the dakhma, or 'tower of silence.' There, the body is exhumed.

"The towers are large, round structures, open to the elements, built in the form of three concentric circles. Male corpses are placed on the outer circle, females on the middle circle and children on the inner circle. Once a corpse is laid out, the vultures take about twenty minutes to strip all of the flesh off the bones. Decomposition is brief, and the physical body, although conquered by death, is quickly returned to the living world by way of the vultures.

"Zoroastrians view the world as being in a constant state of conflict between the forces of good and evil. The all-pervading God of wisdom and righteousness is Ahura-Mazda. His evil opposite is Ahriman. Ahura-Mazda is accompanied by numerous manifestations of his greater whole and also by a series of lesser deities, or angels. In turn, each deity has an opposing evil counterpart. The balance between the two forces is equal.

"According to Zoroastrians, Ahura-Mazda will send a savior and the forces of evil will be banished. But until that time, the struggle between good and evil, purity and impurity will go on.

"As death is the worst sort of impurity, representing the evil work of Ahriman, it is essential that the body be treated correctly. The rapid transition of the body from decayed corpse to a source of renewed life signifies that the triumph of Ahriman is only a temporary, and thus hollow, victory."

Egil slapped him on the shoulder and F snapped out of his trance.

"Well, here we are," said Egil. "Krov-Kala."

They were standing on the eroded remains of the city fortification wall. The sheer scale of the ruins was breathtaking.

All around was nothing but sand-dunes, rolling out majestically and producing a mystical and magical effect on F. The overwhelming impression was one of unadulterated sand and space. The sky above had never seemed so vast. The cobalt that stretched to every point above the compass was accentuated by the grandest of silences. The only sound to be heard, and then, only if one listened closely, was the deep hum of the earth itself.

Surveying the expanse, F momentarily shuddered under the weight of isolation. He felt outside of time, as does the man who suddenly comprehends his mortality and feels the cold breath of the abyss. F stumbled into a hollow emptiness that plunged ever downwards, his thoughts imploded in upon themselves, but he caught himself, and hurriedly searched for the physical assurance offered by his feet on the earth.

For now, F was alive, and life was good.

Within a few days, F became intimately familiar with the effects of living in the desert. The heat made his head swim. His muscles sored from walking long distances in the sand, each step slipping away beneath him, the arches of his feet aching. His skin burned and then tanned, and his body tightened. Each morning F would awake more refreshed and rejuvenated than the day before. Leaving the tents he would scan the glow on the horizon over the dunes and swing his arms with muscular assuredness. He grew in elasticity of movement, and once more felt strong in body and mentally alert and aware.

But out at site, Nikolai cut a sorry figure. His body was all hard edges, all knees and elbows. His frame was skeletal, almost ready for the grave. Egil swaggered up to him, exuding confidence. He sat down beside Nikolai, threw a friendly arm over his shoulder, and gave him a playful hug. Nikolai squirmed in annoyance, pushing Egil away. Egil laughed.

"Well Nikolai, we're doing it," he said, nodding towards the excavations that were taking place before them.

Nikolai shaded his eyes from the sun and screwed his face up. Egil lit a cigarette.

"Yes Nikolai my friend, we are doing it, the dream is alive, and the dream is real. They said we couldn't do it, but here we are, making it work."

He held a finger aloft.

"I have a dream!"

Nikolai flinched in annoyance.

"Egil you are fool, you know not what you say. You just sit here and run dig. I have to meet officials. You not understand. For you it is easy. For me, it is not so easy. You are fool."

"Oh come on Nikolai," said Egil, feeding off the Russian pessimism. "Everything is going great. Look at this site. It's perfect. It's exactly what we had hoped for. When we publish the results you will go overseas. This is going to make you a name. You will give lectures in Paris."

Nikolai hesitated as images of the Louvre appeared before his eyes. He pictured himself speaking to a cultured crowd. Beautiful women surrounded him after the lecture, hoping to share a glass of champagne with the great professor. Dom Perignon of course!

Leading academics implored him to come and visit their departments on sabbatical, all expenses paid. Perhaps they could start a joint venture together? Doubtless the French would have more money than these uncultured Australians. Why yes! This could work. The project was distasteful right now but think of the returns in the long run.

Egil scanned Nikolai's face and observed the change. He continued to talk up a storm about the future of the project, about publishing in this journal and that journal. He reminded Nikolai of the potential for fame and success. Who knew? There was always the private money of the Parsees in Bombay?

"You have to admit, Nikolai," Egil continued. "If this site is what we think it is, and this is some sort of Zoroastrian City, then you are going to be famous."

At last Nikolai couldn't contain his delight. Fame! Finally he would get his dues. In a sudden flurry of arms and legs that sent sand flying in all directions, Nikolai leapt to his feet and earnestly shuffled off towards the trenches.

"Yes, Yes. Egil my friend. We have work to do."

Egil turned to F and laughed.

"Jesus Christ. I tell you it's a bloody miracle that this project is actually up and running. Dealing with that crazy bastard is a full time job."

The Governor of Beruni took a considerable interest in them. Westerners meant money, and they were the only Westerners to be found in his district.

The Governor invited them to the upcoming celebrations in Beruni. A new holiday had been instituted in honor of Abu Rayhan Beruni (973-1048 AD), the mathematician, astronomer and scholar.

On a clear and hot Friday morning, they piled into the back of the truck and rumbled across the desert towards the Oxus River. No one spoke beneath the flapping canvas roof. The bawl of the engine put a stop to that. Although it was early in the day, the air that buffeted the canopy seemed sent straight from the pits of hell.

Outside, the scenery flew by in a blur of sand and salt-encrusted cotton fields. The truck roared over a tarmac road that softened beneath the unrelenting sun, the tires making a slapping-splashing sound as if they were passing over wet plaster.

The cotton was pathetic in places, struggling to grow through the salinized soil. Nearing the Oxus River there was increasingly dense vegetation and the sand dunes gave way to clusters of birch trees.

They passed people walking down the side of the road, old Turkmen wearing knee-high leather boots, their heads crowned by distinctive black and white skullcaps, and high cheek-boned girls with immaculate complexions walking in groups, wearing bright and colorful dresses. As the truck passed by, the girls would catch a glimpse of F and then huddle together, pointing and giggling. F would wave to them and they would wave back, laughing and blushing.

Soon, small habitations appeared with increasing regularity. Individuals gave way to larger parties, until there was a steady stream of Karakalpaks and Turkmen, wearing their heavy chapans in spite of the sun. Everyone was heading into town for the festivities.

They wound through the streets of Beruni until the high walls of the town stadium appeared. They got out of the truck and climbed a steep flight of stairs that led to the interior of the stadium. Armed guards flanked the entrance.

Their position afforded a spectacular view. The stadium was a large, concrete edifice harking back to the Soviet era. They sat in the high-box, where the VIP's could relax in the shade. In the old days this was where the communist party bosses would wave down at the prols. It was just like the news footage of the May Day parades in Moscow, where Stalin, Khrushchev and Brezhnev stood in similar boxes and waved down at the unwashed masses.

When they entered the high-box, they were directed to the front row of seats beside the Governor's chair. Thousands of people milled about below in the bleaching sunlight, their dark features crowned by the ubiquitous skullcap. Men reclined on the concrete stadium seats, covered by their chapans, seemingly oblivious to the heat. Boys and girls roamed about in groups, wearing their best clothes.

Nikolai, Egil and F were left to themselves as the Governor and his entourage attended to other important dignitaries. F observed the crowd for some time. The mouth-watering smell of sizzling shashlik rose up from below.

"Come on Egil," F said. "Let's get down there and grab something to eat."

"No, no," hissed Nikolai. "We are guests of honor! We cannot move."

"Oh horseshit," responded Egil, angrily. "Come on. I'm hungry."

Leaving Nikolai to suffer in solitude, they rose from their seats and descended into the fray. Crowds stretched off in every direction, producing a head-ringing clutter of noise. Traders had set up stalls to sell teapots, shirts, hats, plastic sunglasses and shoes. Old men sat on the ground and laid out random engine parts. Smoke from shashlik vendors filled the air and the sound of crackling fat spattered all around. Above the din, rockets shot upwards and roared into the sky, coming down at random, sending people running for their lives. Wrestlers and dancers moved through the crowd, waiting their turn to perform in the stadium. Rams were led through the seething masses, in preparation for the battles that were about to take place.

Standing in the sun, the sweat running in rivulets down their necks, their shirts sticking to their backs, they ordered flat loaves of naan and skewers of shashlik. Some men were sitting at a table nearby, eating shashlik and getting very drunk. With messy, bleary faces, they shoved cups of vodka towards Egil and F as a token of hospitality. Egil and F pulled up chairs and downed the vodka, all the while squinting through the glare and wiping the sweat from their brows.

It was almost noon and loud roars from the crowd signaled that the celebrations in the stadium had begun. Egil and F made their way back to the high-box and dropped, sated and happy, into their chairs. Nikolai was still sitting in self-imposed martyrdom, unfed and annoyed. Soon, the Governor returned and took his seat. The most important men in the district sat behind him. A fanfare blared out over the PA system. It was time for the games to begin.

The stadium was now full of rams, all primed for the fight. Each ram stood by its master, waiting for the call to come forward. In order to stop the rams from fighting prematurely, each animal was chained to an iron peg, hammered firmly into the ground.

Two of the rams were brought together in the center of the stadium and released. The animals backed away from each other, their steps steady and deliberate. Back, back, back they went, until they were fifty feet apart or more.

And then they charged.

All of the force and strength in their powerful haunches propelled them forward in a headlong gallop that thundered above the crowd. With an almighty CRACK they collided.

As the rams connected, the crowd let out a roar. The rustle of money changing hands could be heard all over the stadium. For a few seconds the rams stood still, trying to reassess where they were and what had happened.

Once the rams regained their senses they backed up for another run. Back, back, back. And then off again! Charging at each other, heads lowered, hundreds of pounds of raw muscle, bone and horn bent on collision and destruction. BANG! They hit with a crunching dull THUNK and again the crowd roared.

Giddily, the rams backed up and did it all over again. The number of times the rams would go at each other was astounding.

Sooner or later, though, one would tire and signal defeat by refusing to back up. The defeated ram would sidle away, looking morose and forlorn, too embarrassed to face the victor.

During these battles F found himself standing up with the crowd, betting with Egil on one ram after another, roaring in approval or cursing in disappointment. Gold teeth glinted and dark eyes flashed. Muscles tensed in apprehension. Senses sharpened with concentration. The crowd milled and hummed and the heat pervaded all.

The PA system crackled again. The Governor stood up before a microphone and addressed the crowd. Thousands of bemused faces looked up. The Governor asked Egil to speak.

Egil approached the microphone, paused for effect, raised his forefinger in a lecturing pose and began to address the crowd. With ten thousand eyes looking up at him, Egil was truly in his element. He looked every bit the dictator. The comparison could not have pleased him more. Egil had always felt that his real destiny was to be a general or a king. He wanted to be an Alexander, a Caesar, a Napoleon.

"Over two thousand years ago Alexander crossed the Oxus," he began.

His voice reverberated around the stadium. The crowd looked up, mesmerized. His poise and words resounded with strength and measure. He lifted the multitude up with passion and charm, moving effortlessly between Russian and Turkmen. The people were entranced, for they were hearing words of greatness.

And with those words Egil could have commanded them to rise up and follow him into battle and conquest, and they would have willingly done so, gaining momentum as an irresistible force, swords held aloft behind the banner of Egil, the Steppic Hordes pouring out of Central Asia, as their forefathers had before them.

And at that moment there was a flash of greatness nothing short of the power of lightning.

A sliver of light escaped from the entrance to Egil's tent. The music grew louder as F approached. F looked in from outside in the dark.

Beethoven.

Egil was standing alone at the drawing table, engrossed in his plans. He hummed quietly along with the music and seemed completely at peace with himself.

But by then the break in their friendship had already been made, and F knew that he would never return and that he would never work as an archaeologist again. He had known it that cold afternoon out at site, when the first Siberian winds had cut into him like a lash, and he had slowly returned to the dig-house for the final time.

Too many years had passed and finally there was the mutual realization that the friendship had passed as well. There could be no room for friendship if *both* men aspired to greatness.

F recalled Egil's words,

"Great Men are above humanity."

Egil had accomplished what he had set out to do. His goal was the work, which he had successfully completed. Egil knew that only the work would be remembered. The work was the honorable contribution, the gift back to the greater brotherhood of humanity.

All else was a mere trifle, the friendships, the arguments, the schisms, none of these things mattered to him. They were unavoidable. They were life itself. So what if people dropped by the wayside?

To the truly great of spirit, friendship was not of any meaningful consequence. Such was the nature of things.

Did not Napoleon forfeit his army in Egypt? Did not Hitler abandon his army at Stalingrad? Did not Alexander murder Cleitus, his trusty lieutenant?

F walked quietly away.

The next morning F got his things together. He had arranged for a car to take him to the Oxus.

When his bag was loaded Egil appeared. They formally shook hands. There was nothing for it.

"See you then," said Egil.

"Yeah. See you," said F.

F got in the car. They both knew that they wouldn't see each other again.

As the car pulled away F looked back and could see Egil standing by the tent. Then Egil turned away. F knew that Egil was looking for something else to do, something to take his mind off the friendship lost. F turned and stared at the road ahead.

The driver was named Usta. Usta was not prone to light conversation. He was a tough old Turkman. He wore a tweed jacket and a porkpie hat. Usta used to turn up at site occasionally, when out shooting hares. When he did speak, it was in a war-like yell. His ancestors had ruled through strength and valor. Let sadness go. Life would go on. There was no room for emotion with Usta. Life was life. You lived and died.

Swinging around a corner, a pack of dogs ran out at the car. One of the dogs, as big as a boar, attacked the front bumper and went under the wheel. The impact felt like they had hit a horse. F looked back over his shoulder and saw the dog lying in the road with a broken back, its head raised in agony.

Usta glanced at F and laughed a loud booming laugh from deep in his chest. It was not a vindictive laugh. He laughed because that was life. Life and death. It was all part of the cycle. Why worry? Why question? Usta had laughed because he saw that F still had so much more to learn. F was no Turkman. No conqueror. Not *yet*. Usta laughed because there was no reason not to. Laughing was good. At any time.

They arrived on the banks of the Oxus. There was no bridge, merely a slap-hazard pontoon, segments of floating iron panels chained together. Usta bid farewell with a simple wave.

Time was on F's side. As he began to cross the pontoon, he felt alone in a very foreign world, a timeless world. Half way across the river he put down his bag and lit a cigarette. He was in no rush to be anywhere.

All around him the churning Oxus flowed by, sluggish and heavy. The immensity of the river was breathtaking. On the pontoon all manner of life trundled by, old men in leather boots and chapans, women and girls in brightly dyed ikat dresses and scarves, Kazakhs with walking sticks, Uzbeks with goats, Karakalpak women with enormous bags of vegetables balanced precariously on their heads.

F thought,

"So this was the world that Alexander saw over two thousand years ago when he had crossed this same river."

F lost himself in the sight of the surging eddies.

"Alexander saw the same swirling, tumbling muddy mass, flowing endlessly, timelessly on. But this river is a force of nature that makes even Alexander's exploits seem transient, pointless and vain."

F looked back across the river to the east. The day was clear and a deep, sapphire sky stretched on into infinity.

And somewhere beyond the reach of his given vision, F detected figures riding through time, conquerors and prophets, rulers of men with voices of Gods, makers of history whose names remained when all else was gone.

And among them F saw Egil, a man worthy of this esteemed company, a man of grand plan and action, a friend and foe, angel and demon, dualistic in nature, representing life in all of its facets, both good and bad and at the same time neither.

F turned to the west and continued his way across the pontoon. He thought of Usta. There was no need to think so much. It was better to laugh.

Autumn

CHAPTER NINETEEN

The Old Man and the Moon

It was the last warm night.

Something prodigious was astir.

The old man could hear laughter and the clinking of glasses from the building on the far side of the garden.

"It must be a Saturday night," he reflected. "They have forgotten me again."

The old man raised his eyes and was greeted by a majestic sight, the moon, sitting plump and full in rich vermillion, above the twilight horizon.

"Ah!" sighed the old man, as he drank in the glorious display.

"Old man!" said the moon. "You are still here. I see you once again sitting in your garden. And sitting outside at night. Have your keepers forgotten you?"

"Yes old friend, my keepers have forsaken me, but I harbor no grudge. I would much rather be left outside to admire you than wheeled into my solitary cell. For you are indeed resplendent tonight, and the air is warm and I am at peace. But there is something else that I discern, I sense a change is coming. There is a new urgency in the air."

"Perhaps your keepers sense this urgency as well?" laughed the moon.

"Ah yes," replied the old man. "But, they are young. Let them be young! Let them drink and laugh and forget about old men. Their blood runs hot. It is the natural way."

"Well then old man," said the moon, "fortunate you are to see me this eve, for tonight I march in grand parade. Have you ever seen such a sight? No less than a transcendental wonder! To shine forth as though gorged from a banquet, to play with tides and tug at oceans as though with puppet strings, now fiery red, now impassioned gold. What joy!

"Ah moon," said the old man, "you fill me with delight! What mysterious powers you have, for not only can you play with the tides, but you cause dogs to howl and cats to fight and also raise something wild in men, though most are too preoccupied to notice."

"Yes," said the moon. "Listen now to the sounds in the house, laughter and merriment. Passions are being stirred by my subtle tweaks.

"But my puppets remain unaware. What a game! And the best part of all is *not knowing* how it will all end. Perhaps angry passions will flare? Perhaps there will be a fight? Perhaps lustful passions will prevail? Perhaps there will be love-making?"

"Great moon," said the old man. "As an old acquaintance of yours I request love-making over fighting."

"Ha!" laughed the moon. "Do you really think my powers reach that far? If they did there would be no place for the random, for the unpredictable, for the twists and turns that lend life mystery."

"Oh moon," said the old man, "you are rising higher up now, up, up into your celestial realms. Continue on your journey. But I most earnestly request of you to strain the passions of love-making on this night. For time passes. Farewell."

CHAPTER TWENTY

The Wasp Suffers from Insomnia

"Curses! Curses!" hissed the wasp as it skirted below the garden canopy to avoid the moonlight.

When flying over the lawn the wasp could even see its own shadow, such was the brilliance of abundant reflection.

"My, my, little wasp," laughed the old man. "What a right old tizz you have worked yourself up into. You are frothing at the bit like a horse that has run the mile. You even have a lather!"

"Oh, old man, do not dare push my buttons this evening. What are you even doing out here? Are not infernal invalids meant to be tucked up in bed by their keepers at this hour?"

The primal grunts and groans of sexual urgency emanated from the far side of the lawn.

"As you can well hear, my friend, I am not foremost in their minds at this moment."

"Yes," jeered the wasp. "They appear to have found friendship in a manner of which you will never indulge."

"Theirs is more than an act of mere friendship," replied the old man. "Their joining is the greatest of acts."

"Ah yes old man," scoffed the wasp. "Friendship and greatness indeed! I detected the thread to your last story, although it shuddered as tenuously as the web of a spider."

"A good analogy, dear wasp, for a spider's web is far stronger than most think, enough to spell the doom for many."

"But now, old man, you speak of a greatest act? You speak of the sexual union of the two? Yet I have heard on the wind that this act is the lowest form of love?"

"Another fallacious lie invented by mankind," responded the old man angrily.

"How so?" said the wasp.

"Eros is derided by the religious and decadent man. But in more noble times Eros soared through the heavens and bestowed gifts of lust upon men."

"And why," asked the wasp, "should lust be so vaunted?"

"Because lust is the primordial force that gives birth to life itself. Lust is the unspoken drive, the unstoppable urge, the manifestation of life, the essence of regeneration. To deride lust is to deride life.

"The sexual act is thus the greatest act, the highest act, the most sacred act, the most necessary act, without which life would cease to be."

"And of those of your kind that deride sex as lowly?" asked the wasp. "What is your pronouncement on them?"

"They are blasphemers against life itself. If only there was a hell for them to go to!"

The wasp once again hovered before the eyes of the old man.

"You judge others old man, just as I will judge you. So speak forth. Tell me of sex, of this greatest of acts!"

CHAPTER TWENTY-ONE

The Seventh Story

When F awoke there was a lot of bustle around him. He blinked and raised his head. The first rays of sunlight were filtering in through the dusty windows. The PA blared inaudibly as the first flights were announced.

F went into the departure lounge, away from the frenetic crowds. Once through, he sat down and stretched out his legs, blearily surveying the scene.

The departure lounge was Spartan, which is not a term the Athenians around him would have appreciated.

Paint peeled off the rudimentary concrete walls. Cracked fluorescent lights hung uselessly overhead. Soot gathered wherever there was a surface.

F pulled his jacket tightly around him. It was cold.

The departure lounge began to fill with people, mostly Greeks. But there were also Egyptians, Copts mostly, the men with crosses tattooed on their wrists. There were also a few other itinerant travelers, a few Westerners, going to Egypt for work, or adventure, or romance, or death.

Who knew?

F studied them. His attention focused on the women. Men were of little interest to him. A woman in a straw hat, with pale skin and short, dark hair, sat to his right. She was older than F.

His eyes moved to another girl, about his own age. He had noticed her the moment she had walked in, tall and elegant, liquid in her movements, tanned and supple, with hair bleached by months spent on Greek Islands.

His mind swooned between sleep and sexual fantasy. His sexual desires almost seemed to drown him, as if submerged beneath a great wave.

As for the girl, she only stared out the window, her thoughts far away.

Finally, mercifully it seemed, the flight was called, and the passengers boarded the plane.

F sat back in his seat. He closed his eyes and fell into a broken sleep, only to awaken when the plane taxied down the runway and left the ground, the wings shuddering under the weight of the fuselage.

Rising up over the Attic horizon F observed the receding ground below. As the plane gained altitude he watched the rocky limestone hills of Athens give way to the glittering azure of the Aegean Sea. The port of Piraeus was left behind them, and as the plane soared south over the Mediterranean the sky cleared and the water below exuded a beauty that F had never seen before, a sea of the most brilliant turquoise green wherever it embraced the isles and shoals.

F thought of all of the history that had passed over those waters. He thought of Persian fleets fighting Greek fleets, of Athenian fleets fighting Peloponnesian fleets, Roman fleets and Carthaginian fleets, Phoenician trading vessels, Paul heading west to Rome, Crusaders heading east to Jerusalem, and even, more recently, Germans heading south to Crete. And now here he was heading to Alexandria, looking down upon it all.

F felt that he too was part of this fantastic tapestry, of an ancient and esteemed line of history, and his life was crossing over and through these earlier lives and events. The thought exhilarated him.

F loved history and that was why he had gone to Greece in the first place. That was also why he was now going to Egypt. In time, this same love would take F to Israel and Jordan, to Syria and Central Asia, and beyond.

F was parched with a thirst for history, and he gained a sense of unparalleled delight when he was finally able to see ancient sites that he already knew like the back of his hand. To see the buildings on the Acropolis and at Delphi and Sparta and Olympia and Mycenae and Knossos, had meant far more to him than a mere glance at silent ruins on an itinerary.

At such times F had felt melancholic that there was no one with him to share the experience, no one with whom he could appreciate the history of a building, the events that led to its construction, of how the architectural features were the end result of long periods of experimentation, how a building in itself could be significant insofar as representing a leap forward in the creative ability of mankind.

F had to savor such moments in quiet reflection, in solitary observation.

He had gazed upon the caryatids of the Erectheum, alone.

As he looked down at the sea and saw the islands passing beneath him, many of which he could recognize and name, he felt frustrated at having to remain silent with his thoughts. How he longed to speak to someone about what it meant to him to see these things, to relate his delight at all that he saw.

On passing above the volcanic caldera of Santorini, with its towering cliffs of black ash crowned by whitewashed villages, he could contain himself no longer. He turned to the person beside him and said, "Look! Santorini!"

"Have you been there?" came a voice.

For the first time F looked at his neighbor. It was the woman in the straw hat.

"Yes," said F. "It's one of the most magnificent places in Greece. Look at how the houses are perched so precariously on the rim of the crater. It's amazing where people live. If that volcano went off, they'd all go sky-high. And that crater doesn't look so big from up here, but it is actually miles across. When it erupted the blast was enormous, one of the biggest in history."

"When did it go off?" the woman asked curiously.

"Back around 1500 BC."

"How do we know?"

"By studying volcanic ash layers in ice cores drilled in the Arctic. It's likely that the blast was so massive that it sent a tidal wave hundreds of feet high far into the Turkish countryside. Down in Egypt it certainly wiped out the Middle Kingdom Empire in the Nile Delta. It's probably the event that led to the Hebrew Exodus."

"What?"

"Yes, you know the tale of Moses parting the sea? Well, before the tidal wave made landfall it would have drawn the water far out to the ocean, before surging back towards the land in a destructive mass. This is probably what the 'parting of the seas' refers to."

The woman shot F a quizzical look.

"No one has ever told me that before, but it makes sense. My father is Jewish and he certainly never gave me that interpretation. But I like it."

F grinned at her and said, "Well, it's not a theory that most people of the book attest to."

She paused and smiled and then she said,

"*Intelligence is a powerful aphrodisiac.*"

F laughed and wanted to say something but had been caught off guard and was lost for words.

He gave her a more focused look. He hadn't taken much notice of her in the departure lounge, although she had noticed him. She thought he was very fresh and handsome and youthful. But F had missed her interest.

But, he saw her now. He looked at her hat. It had a large black band. She was of medium height and had black glossy hair, cut just above her shoulders. Her eyes were black too, large and black, giant wells that seemed to flood over him when she looked at him. She also had large lips that were both too large yet unmistakably sensuous. As F spoke with her, he detected the character and alertness of an intelligent spirit, alive and open and free.

As she leant across him again for a closer look at the receding volcano she brushed against him and he could feel that her breasts were full and well-shaped. Something leapt within him again.

"And why are you going to Alexandria?" she asked.

"I really want to get to Cairo," F said. "I don't know much about Alexandria. It was just cheaper getting a flight there. I wasn't planning on staying there. I was going to go straight to Cairo by train."

The stewardess passed by with the drinks cart and F ordered a gin and tonic. The woman laughed.

"Gin and tonic for breakfast? I haven't seen that in a while."

"But look where we are!" F exclaimed. "We *have* to have a gin and tonic. We're flying over the Mediterranean. It's too wonderful not to have one."

"Well then I should have one too."

They sat talking quietly as they sipped their drinks and watched the sun come up over the Levant, off over the Orient, over the Mohammedan lands beyond the horizon.

F said, "Isn't it fantastic to think that Jerusalem and Baghdad are just over there to our left, Rome is just to our right, while the Pyramids are just ahead of us and the Parthenon is just behind us?"

He was reeling happily in the moment, alive to the joy of his situation, with a drink in his hand and a woman beside him and adventure unfurling itself of its own accord.

"How old are you?" she asked.

"Twenty," he said.

"You speak very strangely for a twenty year old."

F didn't know what to say.

"Why are you going to Alexandria?" he asked.

"To write," she said.

"Is it a good place to write?"

"I don't know. I've never been there. But I've always wanted to go there and feel as if I know the place intimately. Have you ever read Lawrence Durrell? He found that it was fertile terrain for writing. I'm dying to finally see it."

F hadn't heard of Lawrence Durrell and felt embarrassed by his ignorance.

She continued, "As I understand it there is a distinct atmosphere to the place. You are right there on the Mediterranean, but it is the Arab world, the Muslim world, old and far-removed. At one time Alexandria was the Paris of the Mediterranean, full of artists and poets and musicians. It was a place of wealth and exoticism, quite different from the more orthodox religious centers."

Her voice trailed off and F looked at her, aware that she was lost in her own introspection.

"And what are you going to write?" he asked.

She snapped out of her thoughts and turned to him, looking at him squarely.

"I write novels."

"What about?"

"All sorts of things, but mostly relationships, sex, you know, erotica."

Much later, F had realized how these words had rung in his head, repeating themselves over and over again. He had felt like he was slipping on ice.

"How long are you going to be there?" he asked, too quickly.

She paused again, calm and relaxed, and noticed how she had thrown him. She smiled because she realized that he was still very young.

"I have no set period. I am going there for as long as I want to go there. I will find a place to live, somewhere small, in the old part of town. And I will write whatever I feel like writing. I have nowhere else I have to be."

F looked out the window. The sea below stretched off in every direction and the drink had gone to his head. He felt light and truly realized that he had no idea where he was going.

As soon as the plane landed F got a tight knot in his stomach, the excitement borne of the unknown, at what he was to expect once he was on the streets of Alexandria, standing alone amidst the hustle of a chaotic Arab city. He had not given any thought as to where he was going to go or what he was going to do. The only thing he really knew about Alexandria was that the old Pharos lighthouse, one of the ancient wonders of the world, had once shone brightly for the ships at sea.

But Pharos had long since toppled.

And there had also been the library, but the Christians had burnt that long ago.

They stood outside the airport. F planned to go straight to the train station.

"Would you like to share a cab into town with me?" the woman asked. "It will be cheaper."

She could tell he didn't have much money.

The taxi swerved erratically through the traffic, the driver relentlessly working the horn between motioning his exasperation with pinched hand gestures, muttering abuse in a low rhetorical tone.

F stared out the window in amazement at the speed of movement, of life, that passed by.

Egyptians wearing dishdashas dived out of the path of the taxi, whether on foot, on bicycles, or motorbikes. The taxi in turn made way for oncoming trucks, whose drivers unblinking eyes betrayed their belief that they would sooner perish than touch the brake, such is the cavalier attitude of the Muslim, who believes that his mortality has more to do with the will of God, than his own driving ability.

"Inshallah," the driver muttered. "God willing," they would make it to their destination.

F could see it, the transience of his life, as the trucks swept by within inches of his nose.

The woman, for her part, remained beautifully composed. Her coolness impressed F. It seemed to wash over him. Between glancing out the window at the new world that leapt at him from every angle he continued a broken conversation with her. And as he looked at her, he could sense that she was very much a woman, not the girls that he was used to.

She smiled at him calmly.

"I have been living in Europe for the last three years and always wanted to come here. I have studied Arabic and read a lot about the place. It's a dream come true really."

"What were you doing in Europe?" asked F.

"Wasting time."

She gave a brief sigh of resignation.

"Over a man."

She was looking ahead as she said this but quickly turned to F and smiled.

"He was an artist. I had gone to Amsterdam to be with him. But he was no good. Artists never are. He took a lot of heroin and kept promising that he would stop but he never did. Finally, I realized he never would. So I left him."

F had not expected this much information. He was slightly bewildered at the things that the woman would say without even being asked. But he was young and couldn't see that it was obvious to the woman that he wanted to know these things. So she had told him.

"Yes. Three years in Amsterdam. Women should steer clear of artists. I wanted to be an artist myself, a writer. But I ended up wasting time hanging around him and supporting him. It took all of my energy. He was sucking me dry. And then I realized that my life was passing me by as I helped him be an artist, but I wasn't given a chance to be one myself."

F looked at her, this woman, sitting across the seat from him, the sultry air of the Nile Delta hanging behind her out the cab window. Her legs were crossed and he could see that they were good legs, and her waist looked tiny beneath her vibrant breasts. Her lips now seemed voluptuous, passionate and rich.

"Please tell me you are *not* an artist?" she laughed.

"No. I'm a student of archaeology."

"That explains why you know about Greece?"

"Yes, I'm seeing all of the places I have always wanted to see."

"I'm glad you like Greece," she said. "I am half Greek."

"So you are half Jewish and half Greek?"

"That's right."

They were entering the old town now and the buildings of Alexandria began to tower above them. The taxi jolted down the pot-holed streets and into the fray of the traffic. Everyone was on the horn and the noise made it difficult to talk. F felt a little jarred, what with the lack of sleep and the plane-ride, to be in the midst of such a scene. He had never seen anything like it.

The center of town was crowded with people. On either side of the road there were piles of rubbish, and a layer of grime covered everything F saw. Sheep were tied up to lamp-posts in front of butcher shops, right beside the hanging carcasses of their brethren, bleating desperately as they waited their turn for the knife. Fruit-sellers hawked melons to passers-by. Clouds of flies swarmed over their produce. The smell was unlike anything F had ever encountered before, dense and repugnant.

In the middle of town all of the buildings were about ten stories tall and towered above the narrow lanes. Shafts of light occasionally broke through to the streets below, but the general impression was of being in a labyrinthine netherworld, echoing with the sounds of engines and beggars crying for alms. F had no idea where he was.

Then all of sudden the taxi broke through into blazing sunlight and before them was the Mediterranean Sea beneath a seamless sky.

They were on the corniche driving east, with the sea on their left and the old city on their right. A clean breeze blew in from the ocean and F put down his window and breathed deeply. He looked at the woman and she laughed.

"So are you really going straight to Cairo today?" she asked.

"I don't know," F said. "Maybe I should stay a day or two and see the place."

"I think you'd regret not seeing Alexandria. This is one of the great cities of The East, mysterious and magical."

F looked out across the sea.

"Why don't you come with me to the Hotel Acropole?" she said. "It's right on the corniche, just up ahead, beside the Hotel Cecil. You've heard of the Hotel Cecil right?"

F hadn't.

She laughed again, delighted at his youth.

"The Hotel Cecil is famous. It's where Durrell and the rest of the expats used to meet for cocktails and discuss their creative pursuits. It's right on the water."

F winced a little. He thought about his meager budget. She could see him hesitate.

"It would help me a lot if you checked into the hotel with me," she said. "Western women get a lot of harassment in this part of the world. If it looks like we're traveling together, then the men will leave me alone."

F didn't really know what to say. Fate seemed to be sweeping him along.

The Hotel Acropole was haphazard and worn. The building had been exhausted by time, now a mere skeleton of its former self, with subterranean creatures struggling for breath inside. The entrance to the hotel was through a small door on the side of the building. They stepped into an elevator that creaked and clanked unsteadily up to the top floor.

All of the hotels in the old city were on the top floors. The lower floors were where *the people* lived, closer to the street and the flies and the din. But, the top floor was above the smell and the racket.

The woman walked up to the desk and did all the talking, handing over their passports. The Arabs behind the desk leered at the free and immoral Westerners, their derision only superseded by their desperate jealousy.

Other men sat in the lobby, looked brazenly at F, drinking small glasses of sweet tea and smoking cigarettes, speaking softly in the Arabic tongue, something F had never heard before. They reclined on musky furniture that, with the rest of the décor, looked as if it hadn't been changed in the last hundred years. If it weren't for the light coming in the windows, the whole picture would have been one of complete sloth and disregard.

In contrast, the hotel room was very large. F had never seen such a high ceiling in a hotel room and there was an overall feeling of space. Two windows opened to the east and flooded the room with light and clean air, a welcome surprise after being in the lobby.

Two beds sat on the far side of the room, adjacent to the windows. The woman put her hands to her cheeks and said, "It's beautiful!" and ran to a window.

"Look over there," she said, pointing.

F walked over and stood beside her. Before them was the town square, a large open park, with a statue of Muhammad Ali, the Egyptian Pasha, in the center standing on the top of a tall column. Around the edge of the park milled the crowds to the accompaniment of car-horns and the cries of hawkers. And off to the north was the sea, stretching off over the horizon, following the coast to the Levant in a steady, even sweep.

"God, I can't believe it!" she cried excitedly, holding onto the windowsill.

"There's the Hotel Cecil that I was telling you about," she said, pointing to the far side of the park, where another period hotel, somewhat more grand, stood on the corniche.

The woman turned and surveyed the room. One of the beds was larger than the other one.

"This one's mine," she said, throwing herself down.

F's head was spinning with excitement. He sat down on the smaller bed and looked at her. She propped herself up on one elbow, and kicked her shoes off. She stared at him and he at her and neither one said anything for a while.

Then, F wasn't sure what he should do so he reached for his cigarettes and lit one. He leant back on his bed so he could see out the window but also see her and he drew on the cigarette.

"Can I have one of those as well?" she said.

"Sure," he said.

"Will you light it for me?"

F put a fresh cigarette between his lips and lit a match. He drew back and then handed it to her. She took it, smiling at him all of the time.

F could barely contain himself. The tension was stabbing him. He only had to step towards her. He knew that she wanted him to and no word need be spoken, just undress her and fall into the unrestrained, transformative swell of sex.

She stared at him, curiously.

"Have you ever read any Anaïs Nin?" she asked.

"No, I haven't," he said, again ruing his lack of knowledge. "What did she write about?"

"She wrote about men and women and sexual awareness. Her stories are a study of sexual power, and experimentations with the forces of eroticism. They are beautiful to read. Lots of people write about sex. But not many can write real erotica, because erotica goes so far beyond mere sex. Sex is the culmination of eroticism, but eroticism itself isn't just sex. It is a core force of life, and a power of great beauty to be devoured, a current running through us, beneath the entire pretense of the lives we construct around us, just below the surface."

"*Go*," F yelled to himself. "*Just embrace her. Go! What are you waiting for?*"

But he couldn't leap. Something held him back.

Finally, the woman sat up and faced him.

"I'm going to go and shower and freshen up."

She got her things and left. The showers in the hotel were communal and were not located within the rooms. It was an old hotel.

F leant back and stretched out on the bed and looked out of the window up into the pale Mediterranean sky. He kept thinking about her, his body charged. She would be back in a minute. He needed to approach her the moment she walked in the door.

But when she walked in, drying her hair with a towel, F had frozen when she stared at him, so she proceeded to unpack her bag.

The train station opened up before F like something grandly familiar amidst a new and foreign world. The architecture of the building was so strongly resonant of the British Empire that for a moment he felt he could regain his bearings. But once inside, he found that the building was little more than a deteriorating frame in the process of being ravaged by the older, indigenous culture, a vain monument to order where there could absolutely be none.

The platforms were covered with an endless array of orientalia, chickens in cages, men in dirty robes, a plethora of oversized bags and boxes among which children ran and played.

And pervading all was the almost sweet stench of humanity, putrefying, unwashed, diseased and decaying.

"*What could it all mean?*" thought F.

The last train to Cairo had already left so F purchased a ticket for the following day at noon.

All the while the woman hung in the background, more somber and reserved than before. A lot of Arab men approached her. She talked to them easily, but remained aloof.

They left the station and hailed down a horse-drawn buggy.

"I can't believe you are just going to leave Alexandria without even seeing it," she said, as they rolled down the street. "Doesn't this seem fantastic to you?" she asked, with a wave of her hand out towards the city.

"Yes it does," F said.

She frowned.

As the buggy passed down the alleys between the chaotic buildings of the old city F didn't know quite what he felt anymore. He had wanted adventure, and now he certainly had it. But he felt as if he was standing on the brink of an enormous drop, a great fall, and that he was stumbling off the edge. His chest felt tight.

The woman had been intently studying his face as F had stared out the window, bewildered by all that he saw around him. She tried to remember what it had been like when she was his age. Had she been so uncertain, so inhibited and unable to act? Had she run away from that which her senses had so clearly drawn her towards? She couldn't remember. What was it with this boy? He was so free and acutely aware of all he saw, so interested and curious and adventurous. Yet from whence sprang these roots that held him down and wouldn't let him fly?

She leant across and took his hand.

"Well if you are so set on leaving then we should at least go out for a decent drink."

She turned to the driver.

"Foundouk Cecil. Shoukran."

When the buggy broke free of the old city and raced onto the corniche, F again felt the exuberance of earlier in the day. The sun was now low on the horizon and hung over the western side of the Mediterranean in a coppery blaze. A breeze blew off the sea. Cars raced by, freed of the bonds of the old city, and all movement was open and fluid. The woman was looking over at the sun. Her face glowed in the golden light and her eyes and hair shone as black satin.

The stairs of the Hotel Cecil were built of marble and the entrance was grand. F and the woman sat down on the balcony that looked over the sea. A bow-tied waiter took their orders and they sat back and waited for their drinks and smoked cigarettes, feeling good to be out of the morass, in the pure ocean air, in white wicker chairs on a cool marble floor.

"So this is the place where the tidal wave came in is it?" asked the woman, scanning the horizon as the sun dappled the ocean with flashes of gold.

"That's right," said F.

He pointed north to where Santorini lay beyond the horizon.

"That's about where the eruption took place, right over there. The tidal surge would have been enormous, beyond comprehension. If we were sitting here when it happened, the first thing we would have seen was the ocean receding at a rapid rate. The water would disappear over the horizon. But by then it would be too late. The

Delta is so flat that there is no high ground. We would have first seen a distant, watery mound on the horizon. As it approached it would have gained strength, growing in height. And everything for miles inland would have then been obliterated, as simple as that."

F felt very content with this theory because it made more logical sense than any religious explanations.

The woman was leaning forward, clearly enjoying herself.

"But what makes you so certain that it was the same event that led to the exodus? Wasn't that meant to have happened when the Hebrews crossed the Red Sea?"

"That's the common explanation. But in the Hebrew it is quite likely that they referred to the *Reed* Sea, not the Red Sea. The Reed Sea is an area of the Nile Delta, the swampy marshlands. It makes sense that the reference is to that area because the Hebrews were located there. We know they were located there because the earliest non-Hebrew sources that refer to the Hebrews are found in Egyptian records that place them around the Nile Delta."

"So tell me," said the woman, "you base this whole theory of the exodus on a tidal wave and a single mistranslation?"

"No! The beauty of this theory is that so many elements fit together. First, there is the tidal wave. But then there are the biblical references to the Hebrews following a pillar of fire and a column of smoke. These are also references to the volcano. And the passages that describe darkness descending on Egypt, well, that was the ash fallout from the volcano. And the famine that followed was due to the ash destroying the crops. And, these final events are not only recorded in the Hebrew texts, they are also referred to in contemporary Egyptian documents at the end of the Middle Kingdom. Effectively, they refer to the same event. It all makes great sense."

"Go on," said the woman, intrigued.

"All of these factors combine together to form a logical explanation. Undoubtedly, some of the Hebrew accounts were based on real events. The Hebrews were certainly in Egypt. And at some time they did leave. What form the exodus took is another matter. But there was some kind of an exodus. And the beauty of this theory is that because the eruption can be dated through studying ice cores, then we have a good date for these events."

"Is there more?" the woman asked, delighted.

"Yes. You have to keep in mind that the Hebrew texts were not written down until much later, hundreds of years later. These stories were passed down orally, generation to generation, taking on a mythical quality. And when they were finally written down it was by the priests who wanted to reinforce obedience to Yahweh among the Jews. And they did this by giving a religious explanation to events that were simply the product of the physical world."

The woman ordered two more drinks and when they arrived she shifted closer to F, and slipped her hand over his, carefully, so as not to draw attention from the Arabs. She ran her fingers over the golden hairs on the back of his hand, lost in reflection.

Dusk was turning into the true dark of night as they walked along the cornice. The waves crashed onto the rocks below the walkway. The first stars were already out and the wind that blew in from the ocean was warm. The woman had slipped her arm through his and the two of them were walking slowly, close, the wind folding around them.

F and the woman were alone. Away from the street-lights, when no cars were passing, F put his hands around her waist and drew her into him. Her face came up to his, her lips open and ready, and she pressed into his body with her breasts. He could feel them, firm and strong, against his chest, and felt her tongue move languidly over his. Hotness welled up within him and he pulled her into him even more firmly.

When F awoke he was cold. The candle had gone out and he shivered as he realized he was naked on the bed. She was under the covers, somewhere in the darkness, asleep.

F slipped off her bed and moved over to his own beneath the window. A three-quarter moon hung low on the horizon, and as his eyes adjusted he began to recognize the outlines of the room. He shivered and pulled the sheets up to his neck. The room smelt strange, different to anything he had ever smelt before.

He turned on the pillow so that he could face the woman, and he thought of everything that had just happened. She also had the sheets pulled up tight and all he could see in the moonlight was her black hair. Her face lay hidden.

"*I know nothing of her,*" he thought to himself, and for a moment he felt dreadfully alone.

Getting up on his knees he peered over the windowsill.

Below him, the park was outlined in a ghostly dim light. The drooping tops of palm trees stood illuminated in the moonlight but the grass and paths below were lost to sight. The streets that surrounded the park were empty, and he thought that it must be the darkest hour. The shop fronts were closed and all below seemed abandoned and barren.

He looked up at the stars, hanging steadily over the sea, and listened to the sound of the waves, crashing on the break-wall. And then, ever so slightly, other sounds began to filter up from the dark depths below.

At first, F discerned a breathing sound, bordering on the imperceptible, like the sound of an engine from far away, edging in and out of hearing. But then it was unmistakable and F's heart beat faster inside his chest and he froze in fear. And the breathing matched his own heart-beat and grew louder and louder until it turned into curses flying up from below.

It was then that F saw the beggar crawl out of the darkness. F could see that his legs were tiny, shriveled and deformed. The beggar dragged himself forward using his hands. His garbled words, as if from a devil, rose to F's ears before being lost in the deep sky above, the sky that had seen all of those things infinite times before in that ancient land.

The beggar dragged himself off down the pavement, into the dark, pulling himself over the filth of the street on his stomach, so far beyond desperation to even recall such a sensation.

When F awoke, daylight was streaming in the window. The door opened and the woman entered the room. She had showered and her hair was wet, glistening in the Delta morning light. The glow of the morning caught her face and she shined exuberantly, happy and joyful. Her rich, red lips smiled wide and her eyes danced with life.

She approached his bed and in a fluid motion eased onto F so that she was astride him where he lay below the sheet.

Her eyes glowed and her breasts stood out before her, persuasive and alive.

"How are you then?" she asked and ran her hand up his neck to his face.

"Good."

"You OK?" she asked, still smiling, riding her hips firmly over his groin, grabbing his hands and placing them on her thighs.

"Yes. Just tired," he said.

"Well I have something that will wake you up," she laughed.

As she began to remove the sheet he restrained her hand and said, "No."

She stared at him.

"What's wrong?"

"Nothing."

She laughed, thinking he was joking.

"What do you mean?" she smiled.

"I can't explain," said F.

Standing on the platform, F felt numb. It was almost noon. Although moving into autumn the Egyptian heat still weighed oppressively on his shoulders.

F had walked to the far end of the platform, far away from the shade where the Arab travelers lounged on the ground, waiting for the call to board the train. The travelers were subdued by the heat of the day and drearily waved flies from their faces and mumbled amongst themselves, paying little attention to F.

F sat down on his pack and lit a cigarette and waited. He glanced back at the diesel engine, caked with crud, ticking over rapidly in short bursts before returning to a steady idle. His eyes ran back from the engine, past the carriages, and to the shade of the station. Sheets of iron roofing had fallen off, paint had cracked and peeled, and the windows were black with soot.

He turned around and stared up the tracks towards Cairo.

When the call came to board, he waited for the hordes of travelers to get on first. He didn't feel like fighting for a seat. The Arabs boarded the carriages in a fighting, crazed fashion, amidst much yelling and pushing.

F walked past the carriages. Children leant out of broken windows, fighting for air in the unventilated, broken-down boxes, drenched with the stench of tobacco and poultry.

Then he saw her. She was standing in the shadows of the station, some distance away. She had on her straw hat. He stopped and she saw that he had seen her, so she stepped into the light and walked down the platform towards him.

"So, you're really going then are you?" she asked.

"Yes."

She looked away for a while, up the tracks towards Cairo, and then looked back into his eyes. She managed to smile at him. She raised her hand up to his cheek and then ran it through his hair.

"I'm so sorry you're going," she said. "I don't know why you are doing this."

She ran her hand over his shoulder, feeling the curves of his arm.

"But you are still very young. I forget."

She pulled away.

"You'd better go then," she said.

F picked up his bag and got ready to climb up through the door. The woman reached out and held his hand and looked him firmly in the eye.

"I just want you to know that life is short, but it is good," she said. "Don't miss it. Don't let it pass you by."

Then she turned and walked back down the platform and was lost in the crowd.

As the train rattled and swayed down the line, F knew he would never see her again. His gaze rested on the hazy green Delta, and he fought a hollow feeling from deep inside. For in his action and inaction he could no longer discern right from wrong. Yet the essence of nature rung loudly in his head that something great had passed him by, and all he would ever retain of her, despite empty grasps and longings, was the sight of her walking away. And that memory would remain with F as if placed outside of time.

For it was timeless in Egypt, most ancient and eternal.

CHAPTER TWENTY-TWO

The Old Man and the Squirrels

It was a leaf landing on his lap that woke him. But his eyes remained shut. The old man sensed the first cool brace of autumn and realized, that while he was sleeping, one of the nurses had draped a blanket over him.

Behind him was a constant scurrying sound, rich with elation and merriment, but laced with haste, the twitter of squirrels racing up and down the oak tree, gathering and hoarding, automatically, instinctively, without comprehension of terms such as 'summer' and 'winter'.

Their quavering conversation rolled on pointlessly and effortlessly.

"Coming up! Excuse me."

"Certainly!"

"That old man is still sitting there."

"Yes, I noticed. Coming down!"

"Surely his time should have been up by now. He is no more than a hollow shell."

"Nice acorn!"

Bump. Scutter.

"Look where you're going!"

"What?"

Bump.

"You dropped it, scatterbrain."

"I'll get it."

"Old man. Hello! Aren't you dead yet?"

"No. Still here," laughed the old man. "Still breathing."

"Ha! See! I told you he was still going."

"Coming through!"

"Did you hear me? I said he is still going."

"Will you keep your mind on the job please? Just because it's nut-time doesn't mean you have to talk to every nut-job."

Bounce. Knock.

"Gracious! Stay to the right. How many times do I need to tell you?"

"Sorry. Work to do."

"Old man. What's the time?"

"I don't know. Why?"

"Well I think it's past time you were gone. Ha!"

Chip. Cheep. Chirrup.

The largest squirrel called out, "Get back to work, the lot of you. This isn't the time for games."

"God, what a kill-joy. Just lighten up, you control-freak."

"Oi! I heard that. Keep your mind on the job. Can't you see that acorn right behind you? Man o man, how can I work with such idiots?"

"Will you pipe down, I'm trying to come through here."

"Oh. Sorry!"

"By the way, you disordered and unruly mob," called out the old man. "Did I ever tell you I once ate squirrel stew?"

Silence. An immediate halt to all activity.

The old man continued, "I have to say it really wasn't all that good. They say you should eat the bones because they are so small and soft, but I found them rather crunchy and unpleasant. And, of course, there was that gamey after-taste. Yuck!"

Aghast speechlessness.

"Ha! Only joking! Got you all!"

The bustle immediately resumed behind him.

"Coming down. Make way I say!"

"We just lost a full acorn each listening to that old fool."

"Confound you, old man. That was in poor, poor taste."

"Oh, come now my furry little companions," said the old man. "It is good to joke and laugh at all times. After all, is that not your own nature?"

"Beep, beep. Acorn delivery."

Boink.

"Butter-fingers!"

"Hey, that's not nice. No name calling."

"Like that will matter when you are starving in the hole and the cold wind is blowing."

"Agh! So serious all the time. Turn your frown upside-down."

"Agh! Don't spew out those corny sayings. Dreadful!"

"Ah squirrels," said the old man. "I do enjoy listening to you so. You give me great happiness."

"What did he say? What is he blathering on about now?"

"Acorns! Acorns!"

"Do you know why you are so favored in this life, my squirrels?" asked the old man.

"Who are you? Socrates?"

"Ha! Because your brains are so small you forget everything instantly. You can never be angry for long and can never harbor a grudge. Surely you are blessed."

"God, when will that old man just put a cork in it? Isn't there some sort of kill-switch that will just shut him down?"

Jerk, jolt, jostle.

"And fear, little squirrels, what of fear? You move as if frightened all the time. But you are not really frightened. Just restless! Fortunate indeed."

One of the squirrels leapt effortlessly from the tree and landed on the lap of the old man.

"Look old man, we like you, we really do. We think you're a nice old bloke. But I do fear one thing."

The old man was baffled.

"I am flummoxed little friend. For surely I am the wisest man of all, and I am certain that squirrels know nothing of fear. What is this one thing that you fear?"

"I fear, old man, that you will not ever BE QUIET!"

CHAPTER TWENTY-THREE

The Wasp Accuses the Old Man of Cowardice

The old man awoke to the sound of geese flying overhead.

He marveled in wonder and joy as they flew in a delta formation, gliding effortlessly south to escape the oncoming cold.

And on that bracing wind, the wasp hovered unsteadily before the old man.

"So, it appears old man that I am not alone in desiring that you hold your tongue. For no-one likes to listen to the ramblings of the mentally infirm. Do you not see your hypocrisy, old man? For how could you be the greatest of men when you fled from sex like a cowardly priest? Some lothario you turned out to be. That story was more a tale of fear than of sex."

"An astute observation!" complimented the old man.

"Old man, I like to hear about your fear. I like to hear how your fear accompanies you like a shadow on the fly-blown streets of Alexandria."

"Ah wasp, there you go again with your poetic turn of phrase. And what is it about streets that conjure up these images? Is it again the great romance of movement?"

"Stay on track old man! Don't drag me down with your divertive ramblings! Your words border on the insane."

The wasp spat in disgust.

The old man fell into his thoughts, as in a trance. Then he spoke, as if from a great distance,

"Who is to say what is sane or what is insane? For is it not insane to assume sanity?"

"What on earth are you blathering on about now?" asked the wasp.

"Well, let us just say, to serve as an example, that a woman is beaten by her husband every day for thirty years. And the husband lords it over her like a dictator, and she has to serve him like a slave, and no matter what she does he beats her anyway. Her life is nothing but a series of beatings, year after year. Until, one day, she can take it no longer and she kills him. Then she skins him and hangs his hide up just like his suit, just like he had always demanded she hang his suit all those years. Then she cuts off his buttocks and cooks them and serves them for dinner at exactly the time he had always ordained that dinner must be served. And this woman is captured and declared to be insane. But is she *really* insane?"

"Ach, old man! My head aches with the pointlessness of your words. Were you not meant to be speaking of sex?"

"And thus I did, dear wasp. But how can one speak of that most powerful and urgent force of nature without a degree of fear? For is there not, in that most heightened moment of human abandon, a transformation from the sane to the insane? When the shackles are thrown off and wild beasts couple in tumultuous frenzy, where is sanity then? When a sharp turn is taken off the familiar paths of daily existence and something deeper and inexplicable rises up within us, something utterly primitive and elemental? Is there not something fearful in this return to beasts? Do these actions not bear thinking about without demanding questions of sanity and insanity and the nature of each? Can the nature of sanity be confronted without trepidation and fear?"

"Ah, old man," said the wasp. "Finally you have a subject you are qualified to speak of. For if ever a man was insane, it is you. So impart your wisdom, oh greatest of men! Speak to me of insanity. But make it sane!"

CHAPTER TWENTY-FOUR

The Eighth Story

Siegfried. F knew it was him straight away.

Standing on the far river bank his profile was unmistakable. Siegfried was instantly recognizable, even from great distances, on account of his tanned crown and grey unkempt beard, but even more so for his posture, that of the archetypal man-child, standing tummy out, lost in thought, gazing at the surging brown torrent that tore by.

And my how the river surged!

Churning and roaring in full-blooded flood, eighty feet high and stretching clear across the valley. All the crops were under water and dismissed in the minds of the farmers, because it was already too late. The farmers, who were wise to the land, knew that there was no point in regret. So they stood and drank in the sheer majesty of what they beheld, for they knew that it was nature.

Monumental. Epochal.

F stood on the edge of the flux and marveled at the sight of gigantic gum-trees being dragged under the surface, deep into the guts of the beast, before being spat out like mere twigs, soaring clear through the air.

He swooned at the magnificence of the sight, so truly terrific, as if the hand of God had showed itself and said,

"Behold boy! What you see is nature and it is grand."

F remembered how some people from the town had not believed that the river could rise eighty feet. But the old farmers knew what the river was capable of and so had built their houses above the eighty foot mark.

And as if in testament to such power, F recalled walking down the road once the river had dropped, seeing chairs lodged in the tops of the gum-trees, far above his head.

F let his gaze drift across the flood to the far bank once more, and there he was again. Siegfried, lost in a trance, watching the remains of a shed being carried by.

Then there was the sound of a gunshot and both Siegfried and F looked up.

In the darkness, just off the side of the porch, Old Ed Mason could hear the dogs chewing away at the dead kangaroo. F heard the gunshot that afternoon and knew immediately what it meant.

Every few days a blast from Old Ed Mason's twelve-gauge would echo up and down the valley, signaling to everyone in the top end that Old Ed Mason wasn't dead yet.

Old Ed Mason, born in the top end, would die in the top end.

"When you don't hear the gun boy, then you'll know I'm dead. Then come and get me and stick me in the ground."

The reality was that every few days Old Ed Mason shot a kangaroo for food for his dogs. Old Ed Mason never spent so much as a brass razoo on a can of dog food. When his dogs needed a feed, he just blasted away a kangaroo. It had always been that way.

"But I'm not dead yet!" he said out loud. "Am I boys?" he called out to the dogs.

The dogs stopped chewing for a moment and briefly raised their heads before resuming their meal.

Old Ed Mason took a long swig of beer.

"Was that you this afternoon boy? Jumping on the floorboards of the old shed?"

"Yeah," said F. "Could you hear me all away over here?"

"Yep. I may be ninety but I ain't dead yet."

"Yeah it was me alright."

"Anything much left of it? It must have been right tore up by the flood?"

"Just a section of the floor. It sort of springs up and down when you jump on it."

Old Ed Mason smoked and fell back deep into his thoughts. He remembered when they built that shed, all those years ago, and how it had served as a sort of communal meeting hall for the farmers, thrown together really, located in the flood-plain, not built to stand the test of time.

A collage of images passed before him.

Old Ed Mason is only a boy. The shed is being built by the farmers near a lagoon, a backwater of marsh, home to birds and snakes, herons and black swans, pelicans and galahs, sulfur-crested cockatoos, and even the rare black cockatoos that sat high in the gum trees, tearing them apart with their massive beaks.

The boy, Ed Mason, has climbed a mountain and looks down at the farmers, hard at work.

"The things that adults do!" he thinks in wonder.

Ed Mason the boy holds a deep aversion to such things. These inventions of man, these shackles imposed upon man by man himself. To young Ed Mason it is all beyond the absurd! What is this shed? What is this house? What is this church? What is this school?

Why are these things?

These are actions beyond comprehension for Ed Mason, the boy.

Time passes. Ed Mason is a bit older now, not a boy anymore, yet not quite a man either. He is inside the shed, men only, no wives, and it is summer and there is beer and whisky and a fat Madame, a hardened old boiler, with red satin dress and cigarette holder, yelling out, "Settle down, settle down! Two lines you bloody animals, the blonde to the left and the brunette to the right."

And young Ed Mason had lost his that night.

More time passes and Ed Mason is a man, a farmer. He is in the shed again. Mulrooney's boxing troupe is passing through and every cove for miles around has ridden in to drink and fight.

"One night only! Go three rounds with the black and win a pound!"

Again, there is beer and whisky and the man's world, the thundering stentorian cry of Bacchus and all that is wild.

And when it had been his turn, he felt fear at first, and he realized that it wasn't the fear of losing a fight so much as fear of losing face in the top end, how he had to win, and how his fear was diminished by pride and translated into anger and fired by whisky.

But then he is ducking and weaving. There is the flurry of red leather. He searches for an opening. Then he is in there fast, quick as a snake, wrangling up against the wall now, breathing hard, and Ed Mason, the man, attacks like a frenzied animal and his opponent goes down. The shed sways to the pitch of the drunken furor.

From that moment on, Ed Mason, the man, can forever hold his head up high in the valley.

When Old Ed Mason heard the boy jumping on the floorboards, it was as if the valley itself was reverberating with the life of his memories and singing to him across the mountains,

"Remember these things Old Ed Mason, for they are you."

When Siegfried moved into the top end he was not alone. There were three of them.

The second was an older man. The third was an older woman. They were Siegfried's parents. They were German. To the local farmers they were seen as the ultimate outsiders.

Because they were.

F remembered the old man, fat as a bull, with a grey moustache and a heavy tan. The old man waddled about wearing only a pair of shorts and a Greek fisherman's cap. His belly was enormous, almost perfectly round, but his legs were relatively lean, almost like sticks.

If you had put a picklehaube helmet and jack-boots on him, he could easily have passed for Bismarck or Hindenburg.

The old man would sit on the verandah and peer through the trees down towards the valley. He played a violin. He liked to amble about at a leisurely pace with a bottle of beer in his hand, one of those old dark brown glass bottles. The old man also smoked cigars.

In the opinion of F's mother, these traits made him a thoroughly unwholesome character. Beer and cigars *and* a German to boot! Not good traits to have if you wanted to be in the good books with F's mum!

F liked the old man, happily playing his violin and drinking his beer.

F and the old man took the dogs down to the river on hot summer days. They sat in the shallow waters as the dogs swam. The sun beat down on their shoulders, and F would try not to laugh on account of the sight of the old man, who looked akin to a hippo cooling itself in a swamp.

The old man cheerfully regaled F with the most florid details of his sexual exploits from back in his younger days. He told F about girls from all of the exotic countries around the world, Swedish girls, Spanish girls, Danish girls, Brazilian girls, and how he had indulged in the most fantastic orgies with these, apparently desperate young women, all in the physical prime of life, ripping their clothes off for the privilege of being serviced by him. The old bull!

But who was F to question? F didn't know what was possible and what was not.

So F sat there happily in the warm water and let the old man rattle off the stories.

Naturally enough, there was a lot of gossip in the valley about the three strange Germans.

The most commonly circulated rumor was that Siegfried had been on some sort of wacky drug bender in 'the city' which had pushed him over 'the edge', into the realm of insanity.

For, it was commonly accepted, as opposed to speculated, that Siegfried was certifiably 'insane'.

It is true that even the old man insinuated this about Siegfried.

"Ja, Siegfried is a yoozlez piece of shit," he would say, cigar in mouth. "He juz zits zere in ze haus unt lizzens to zem muzika, day after day, mein gott, it vill never stop. Ja, he ist ein yoozlez piece of shit. Vot ist der verd for it? Nutcase? Ist zat how you zay it? Ja. Siegfried is a nutcase. Ah vell," he would sigh, "let him be ze nutcase. Who cares ja?"

The first time F met Siegfried, he ran smack-bang into him as he was heading down the drive. Siegfried, with leaves and twigs in his beard and on his clothes, was standing there with a book in his hand. Siegfried was wearing an old, torn sweater, in spite of the heat.

F stood there in slight shock. Siegfried, however, snapped his heels to attention and formally introduced himself.

Siegfried held out the book for F to see.

The book was full of sheet-music, each sheet very complicated, not showing your typical treble and bass clefs, as with piano music, but showing fifteen or so clefs, each representing a different musical instrument.

Siegfried explained.

"You zee, zis clef represents ze violins. Zey start here, la la la, you zee? And zen after ze vorth bar ze cello comes in, ja? And gradually ze other instruments are added. Here is ze brass coming in mit forte forte power ja, da da da da? Und ze bassoon here for ze added power in ze bass," and so on.

"But what do you want?" asked F, bewildered.

"Oh!" said Siegfried, as if waking from a dream. "I vant to play ze piano. I hear you have a piano? I need to practiz to be ze conductor you zee?"

As they walked to the house, Siegfried explained things to F. If Siegfried was going to fulfill his destiny, he needed to practice. Every minute of every day he needed to sit and listen to music, uninterrupted, with the sheet-music in his hands, so that he was so familiar with every piece of music that he could earn the right to hold the baton and guide the musicians with the necessary required skill.

His destiny, he explained to F, was a great burden, but there was nothing he could do about it.

"Destiny iz destiny. A person has a duty to see their destiny fulfilled.

"Failure to do so is to fail in life itself."

F showed Siegfried the piano and left him be.

When F returned that evening, Siegfried was still there, feverishly playing, completely engrossed in earnest concentration.

With a series of formal bows and a circuitous explanation of how F was helping Siegfried in his endeavors to such a degree that he was going to dedicate a performance to F, Siegfried finally wandered off into the dark.

Siegfried continued to come and go in his usual discombobulated fashion of apologies, thanks, and explanations of the process being undertaken that was going to catapult him to greatness.

"Zis is all necessary you zee. How fortunate for ze man vizout destiny, to *not* haf to strive for greatness. But how much *more* fortunate for ze man of destiny, for hiz life has great purpose. Yet vot a difficult road to travel vor such a man, vor to fail makes life a most terrible travail. Success is imperative."

Then, as abruptly as he first appeared, Siegfried stopped coming over.

Late one evening, F's ears pricked up like those of a dog. Coming in and out of hearing were distant breaking sounds.

"Germans," his mother mumbled.

F snuck up the mountainside in the moonlight and followed his way along to the ridge above Siegfried's house.

F suddenly stopped.

Scattered over a wide area were hundreds of broken vinyl records, strewn violently and randomly among the rocks.

F bent over and picked one up.

'Beethoven. Symphony Number 7. Berlin Philharmonic.'

He walked on and picked up another.

'Wagner. Tristan. Bayreuth. 1975.'

And then,

'Rachmaninov. Piano Concerto Number 4. Ashkenazy. London Philharmonic.'

As he searched through the wreckage, F heard raised voices drifting up the hillside from down near the house. F crept through the bush and the voices grew louder, until he could see the old man and Siegfried arguing around a camp-fire, the old man with a half drunk whisky bottle and his violin, pointing the tip of his bow at Siegfried, who stood directly in front of him, glaring and glowering with rage.

Siegfried had a book in his hand and boxes of other books were strewn around him. The fire was crackling away, and Siegfried's enraged expression bore a devilish visage in the sparks of the flickering flames.

The old man was mocking Siegfried, sometimes in German, sometimes in English, but enough for F to know what was happening.

"Great philosopher. Ha! Look at you, a madman in ze boosh. And you have zumzing to add to ze corpus of knowledge? Ha! My only son a stoopid nihilist!"

Siegfried frantically rifled through his books, searching for some quotation, something to back him up.

"You do not even deserve my verds!" he said. "You are too lowly. You are zo blind zat you zink I am a nihilist, when I am the very opposite, for I am the true embracer of life. I say ze holy 'yes' to life. But you!" Siegfried spat in disgust, "You soil yourzelf with your religion and are a sheep ven you should be a lion."

Then Siegfried ran off to get another book from somewhere, and the old man took a deep swig from the bottle and proceeded to pick up Siegfried's books and throw them into the fire.

And when Siegfried returned, he stood frozen, momentarily in shock, before letting forth a roar like a wounded beast. Siegfried picked up the wood-axe, and the old man hurriedly retreated into the bush. But Siegfried was lost in a pure blaze of fury now and was swinging away at trees, screaming, "First my records and now my books? You vant to go the vay of the ze dead, then let zis be! You preach departure from zis life, zen depart! You are not worthy of zis life!"

And F had run away into the dark of the night for fear of what he was seeing and hearing.

A long time passed. Siegfried stayed in the house like a hermit and was rarely ever seen.

Then one brisk autumnal afternoon, as F was running up to the rows of poplar trees from the lagoon, he found himself suddenly face to face with Siegfried.

Siegfried was standing in the middle of a row of poplars, the grey branches forming a grand ceiling above his crown. Siegfried stood as still as a stone, like an effigy on a tomb in a cold, Gothic cathedral. He seemed as if in a trance, but slowly his eyes focused on F.

F stood there, motionless, in fear.

Siegfried studied F's face and then said, "People zink I am insane. Tell me, do you also zink me insane?"

F looked at Siegfried.

"I don't know?" he said.

"Ha! A vise anser. Ze only correct anser!

"*Vor vot ist sane? Vot ist insane? Who is to say?*"

CHAPTER TWENTY-FIVE

The Wasp Feels the Cold

The wasp was huddled up tight against the cold, hunched upon the left shoulder of the old man.

"Why wasp old friend! I didn't even know that you were here. Look how you curl up for comfort upon my shoulder. What could this mean? Are we now friends?"

"Don't be absurd, old man. I am braced against the cold. I am sapped of energy. I can't tell what it is. But my reserves are not so low that I still can't finish you off."

"Ah yes, dear me, I had forgotten," sighed the old man. "You would like nothing more than to be the catalyst of my demise. For that is your nature, and all of nature, good *and* ill, must be embraced if life itself is to be embraced. For even the benevolent life-giving sun, if it were any closer, would malevolently destroy us.

"Or do I speak untruly, for could not the sun be simply ambivalent?"

"Oh yes," spat the wasp in mockery. "I had forgotten. You are the greatest man on earth, for no less than the sun told you so."

"Indeed. And perhaps you are the coldest wasp on earth? Do you not know, little wasp, what message is borne to you aloft on frigid puffs?"

"What?"

"This zephyr is a harbinger for you. It signals the coming of the end."

"Don't speak to me of such things old man," hissed the wasp. "Your words chafe me so. Don't speak to me of death when I hold yours in my tail."

"Little wasp, even if I go before you, we will still go the same way."

"Don't threaten me with an eternity spent with you!"

"Dear wasp, the truth is this, even the sun shall one day die, as will every other sun, for that is the way of nature. But in death there shall be renewal, and that death shall be as natural as birth. I repeat to you, dear wasp, we shall go the same way."

"Agh! Enough!" cried the wasp. "Do you not fear for your own destruction old man?"

"Destruction!" laughed the old man. "No, I do not fear for my own destruction. In fact, the opposite is true,

"For I am a lover of destruction!

"How could I claim to be the greatest of men otherwise? Without destruction there is no renewal.

"And wasp, hear this! Not only do I know something of destruction, my knowledge was won through hard experience. Indeed, I have wallowed in destruction up to my neck! I have wreaked unimaginable destruction with mine own hands. I have created horrors that most people, if they saw such things in a nightmare, would have further nightmares and turn insane!"

"Ah yes," said the wasp, "insanity."

"Or sanity," said the old man, "depending on your perspective. For one man's sanity is another's insanity, and who can say who is right and who is wrong? For just observe the act of destruction as borne by the hand of man. The crowds cry out,

"Insanity!

"They demand a head on a platter! But their real motive is fear, fear of destruction, and fear that sanity lies within. For although they look away, they can sense deep within that destruction is most intimately bound with the sanest nature of things."

"Most pompous of men," cried the wasp in anger. "Your claims are preposterous! Speak then about this destruction. Explain yourself!

"Yes wasp, as you desire!" said the old man. "But listen closely for herein lies a key, however abhorrent my tale may be to the weak of heart."

CHAPTER TWENTY-SIX

The Ninth Story

Turn away from me now, oh you fickle and kind,
Turn away from me now, oh ye of small mind,
For the meek shall not inherit the earth,
And the last shall be last and the first shall be first,
Away with your pity, for pity's sake!
Such shame I revile. You do I forsake.
For now is the time to destroy and to shatter,
Let me slice and cut to the bone of the matter!

The God, when a boy,
Had shone brightly with life,
Like a furious blaze,
He had reveled in strife,
And in all that was evil,
And in all that was good,
Yet he found most pleasure,
In the misunderstood.

In nature, of which he was truly a part,
He saw all of movement,
He saw all of art,
He sensed a great spirit in the wild undergrowth,
To life, he avowed with most solemn troth,

Ah life my sweet bride,
I do truly thee wed,
In wild ecstasy we shall lie in our bed,
And I shall take you,
And you shall take me,
And in birth and in death we forever shall be.

So life did embrace him,
With wine she did ply,
And she bore him aloft,

He looked down from on high,
He lived on the peaks,
And the summits and soared,
For in all honesty,
And in truth,
He went forward.

On his way he confronted,
All in man that is ill,
And he battled head-on,
And defeated with skill,
All of man's sick inventions,
Forced on man by himself,
He most eagerly sought for,
He hunted with stealth.

When he met with religion he had cried,

Blasphemy!
How dare you scorn life and all so dear to me!
I will not hear lies of redemption for man,
Of man being soiled, and dirty, less than
All that he should be,
No less than a God!
A Pan playing pipes,
With hooves left unshod,
Dionysius or Bacchus,
These Gods I call mine,
These do I bow down to,
These Gods most divine.

So he warred with and conquered,
All fallacious claims,
And his dreams remained boundless, unhindered, unchained,
He strode forth in glory,
His actions bore creed
To how life should be loved,
Most cherished indeed.
He embraced the all
That in life was most grand,

He found friendship and greatness
Held in but one hand.

He ran to and ran from and ran back again,
To sex, most mysterious idol of men,
He found there euphoria,
Greatest fear, greatest lust,
In progenitors urging,
A seed grown from dust,
Very essence of man,
Forced forth from the core,
Oh most honest action,
Truth pushed to the fore,
In rightful position,
Sex he did place there
On high pedestal,
Most noble and fair,
A gift to be cherished and loved and adored,
To be thus devoured,
Man's greatest reward.

So this God he marched onwards
In wisdom and wonder,
And all that was sickly
He did rend asunder,
He laughed in the face of the sane and insane,
For here he detected a childish game
Of man's limitations,
Of perspective and words,
Of the infinite angles from which to observe
Finest nuance in man,
Joy in the absurd.

Thus with knowledge on high
Did this Bacchus God roam,
Reckless and wild
Into the unknown,
Where fate brought him to face
The uppermost sight,
The highest of beauty,

She, his crowning delight.

No ear deserves
To hear her name spoken,
That honor reserved
For this God,
His gold token.

But he will tell you this,
Of her hair fair and fine,
Of her kisses of nectar,
Far above the divine.
Where the Gods on the summits
Their faces did turn,
For her beauty incomparable
Their eyes it did burn,
For perfection is brighter than brightest of bright,
Scalding and white,
Most blinding of light.

When she looked at him,
He did not turn away,
And though she burned brightest
His gaze did not sway,
Instead he held steady
In the eye of the sun,
She detected no fear,
He would never run,
For his strength was unmatched.
He was untamed and bold,
A wolf amongst sheep,
Lording over the fold.

In this moment she danced,
For here she had found
Man as a God,
Unrestrained and unbound.
So they merged together,
They fused, became one.
And together they reveled,

And they danced in the sun.

Some say that time passed,
They could never have told.
Time meant nothing to them
In their halcyon hold,
Swimming in love,
Oh most pure and sublime,
Only measured in lightning,
And thunder in kind.

But then came a day
When heaven did turn,
Flung apart from its axis,
Into hell, it did burn.
For all that is worst in man most pernicious
Appeared with all malice,
Acerbic and vicious,

For the lowest of men,
Of most envious kind,
Took sight of the queen and thought her so fine
That with cruel avarice he stole her away,
And had her, then killed her,
Then he ran from that day.

And 'tho he did run,
As a coward runs fast,
The rage of the Bacchus,
He could never outlast,
For Bacchus in torment
Did wail and did scream,

I will cross every ocean
To avenge my queen.
I will search every land
Of the meek and the low,
No stone left unturned,
Enraged I will go
In search of my prey.

A victim I seek,
I will tear like a gale,
Through the lands of the weak.

So in time the final of days it did come,
The man in his grasp,
No more could he run,
He quivered and grimaced and this did he say,
As he cried out for mercy on his judgment day,

Oh Bacchus, most mighty and furious God,
I beseech thee show mercy,
My head it doth nod
In submission,
I plead now,
Impassioned for pity,
I beg now forgiveness.
I lie prostrate before thee.

But savage and raging Bacchus did speak,

Mercy and pity bestowed on the weak?
Forgiveness you ask for,
These things do you seek?
You deal with the wrong God!
You small-minded fool!
For your crime you shall pay,
For your blood I do drool,

And it will not be quick!
I do hereby assure you!
You shall suffer great torments
In this life as none 'fore knew
Could ever be suffered,
Could be thus inflicted,
By one on another.
My will is vindictive
And thirsty
For pain and the sound of your cries,
Music to mine ears,

A balm for my eyes,
Burned by the tears
That dropped where my queen lies.

And this Man become God,
Who can say which?
Unleashed his revenge,
Without blink or flinch.
The torment of his victim
Was most long indeed,
And torture inflicted
Most gruesome to see,
For yea did he suffer
To greatest extent
Atrocious atrocities
Of sinister bent.

Can he resist thus telling the tale?
Of fury so hideous in every detail?
Of the breaking of knuckles,
Of the pulling of nails,
Of the one-thousand cuts,
Of the use of the flail,
Of the flaying alive,
Of the slow disemboweling,
Guts dragged out from inside,
Of the cries and the howling.

Every slow torture invented by man,
See the lips sliced off?
Then fried in a pan?
Before the man's very eyes
That in time would be plucked,
Of knees smashed to pieces,
And the marrow thence sucked.

Of the bones that were broken,
Each one at a time,
Or the flaming red poker,
Application of lime,

Macabre inventions of diabolical minds,
In these Bacchus did revel,

Revenge Is Now Mine!

And when all was done,
And the man was no more,
For Bacchus left nothing,
He destroyed to the core,
He felt no remorse,
And of guilt not a care,
For his queen was avenged,
Oh so white and so fair.

And he no longer railed
But now set out again
And embarked on his trail,
In the low lands of men.
As he wandered now aimlessly,
Hither and yon,
He no longer smiled
But he sang a sad song,

My Queen, My Queen, My Queen you have gone,
And 'tho vengeance is mine,
Still for you I do long,
In my mind you will live,
You, I never will share,
My dear, my sweet, with the finest fair hair.

In this life I must travel
Till the end of my days
And now I have seen
Each and all of men's ways,
From the good to the bad and to all in-between,
From the sane to insane,
To birth and death of dreams,
Full cycle I've come
And yet I remain
The greatest of men

But their ultimate bane.
From this point on out,
No more words shall I utter,
No more to converse
Not even a stutter.
Do others deserve,
Oh most lowly of men!
Your pity, your mercy, I hereby condemn!

Bacchus has grown solemn,
Thus he shall stay,
He shall sit in the sun
As the days run away.
Wisdom shall remain
His only consort,
Granting him solace,
A measured comfort.
But rejoicing in life,
He shall always remain,
Despite his great loss,
Despite his great pain,
He has lived a full-cycle,
And all in-between,
Of a life,
But a beautiful shade of a dream,
He knows all is connected,
And he knows that in death
Will be regeneration,
When he breathes his last breath.

Winter

CHAPTER TWENTY-SEVEN

The Wasp Speaks with the Murderer

The old man was in his chair beneath the tree and the nurses had wrapped him up tightly in a blanket.

The sky above was vivid, translucent. The air was still and the sunshine filtered down through the branches, now stripped of their foliage, onto his face and front, warming him, one of those perfect days of early winter, roborent and bracing.

"Look at me, cold little wasp," chuckled the old man. "I am as warm as a cocoon. I was once but a humble grub but will transform into an angelic butterfly."

"Oh God," quivered the wasp from the old man's shoulder. "This is a new low, even for you."

"I wonder what color I shall be?" the old man mused. "A miracle of verdure? A cerulean sapphire? But of course!" he exclaimed. "I shall be all colors! No less than a chimera-butterfly that floats with utmost grace."

"Again?" spat the wasp. "You sit here all day and still don't even know that there is no such thing as a butterfly with all colors? Tell me, do you see little rainbows flittering about?"

"Oh wasp," sighed the old man. "Let me explain, for these words seem beyond your grasp. Do you not know that the source of all color is the same? A mere child knows that if you spin a rainbow-wheel it becomes white? That colors come from a single source? And although we see colors that separate and delimit, these are products of the physical world of which we too are a part?"

The wasp was riled and creaked to its feet and thrashed its wings.

"And this, no doubt, was the meaning to your poem? That even destruction has a place?"

"But of course, dear wasp. That is the most difficult lesson to learn, and the one that most people are too cowardly to admit, but destruction not only has a place in the nature of man, destruction has a place in the nature of life."

"Wait, old man," hissed the wasp. "For I see you now for what you are, a sadistic murderer! And I am beginning to understand why you are in this place, to escape being caught!"

"As usual, little wasp, you are both right and wrong. There are different motives for murder. The first killed out of lust and envy. He gave no thought to my queen. He acted purely for his own gratification. But when I caught him, I killed him out of revenge. He destroyed my love, and in the process forfeited his own right to live. I killed for vengeance. I killed for retribution. And he felt the full weight of my rage, a terrible thing to behold! But my actions were no more terrible than any horrors perpetrated by the religious and the righteous. And my terrors, at least, may be justified."

"But surely, old man, this is why you are in this place? So as not to be caught?"

"It is true that it is difficult to be caught if no-one knows who you are or where you are from or even where you have been. So yes, dear wasp, I found that the perfect place for me was right here, beneath this oak tree in a garden for the insane. For after my vengeance there was nothing left to say to other men. There were no more words to speak because no men possess the courage required to hear them."

"So you came here to….wait?"

"Indeed wasp. I came here to wait, to wait for our time."

"Our time? Again you speak of *our* time?"

"Ah wasp, do you not see the season? When will the first snowflakes fall?

CHAPTER TWENTY-EIGHT

The Old Man and the Owl

The old man heard the clink of cutlery from across the darkening yard. Dinner was being served. He put it out of his mind. Being seated with the drooling and toothless was no great joy.

"Hopefully they will forget about me this evening," he said. "And what an evening it is. The sky is dark and the wind blows hard. Leaves fall now with a frantic zeal, eager to break free and fly and die. They are as bats, flittering hither and yon, black against the blackening sky, as black as the blustering trees, no more than silhouettes, apparitions. For winter is coming."

"Winter is here," said a voice, low and hollow, trailing off in somber song.

The old man spied a strange shape, perched on the fence, with horns like a devil.

"What is this?" asked the old man directly. "Name yourself. Are you an incubus? Does the reaper come?"

"No old man," came the reply. "Your time has not yet come, but your time draws close and your eyes are opaque."

"My eyes, maybe, but my mind is pellucid right up till the end. For now I recognize you *bubo virginianus*."

"Ah, a man of learning, a man of wisdom, a Solomon. What? Am I to be grateful for the name your kind has bestowed upon me? A bubo? A term of plague and painful death? I prefer my more common name."

"Great horned owl," laughed the old man. "Greetings! And greetings sincerely meant, for you are a grand bird indeed, imposing and strong, impressive in your silence and mystical in your call. For which of my kin do not stop to listen to the grave beauty of your voice? Your call affects the thoughts of a man. In an instant he stands on the brink and considers the shortness of his span and the relentless approach of his destiny. And he thinks of spirits and ghosts and death in the darkest hour."

"Poor and fickle mankind," hooted the owl. "Surely you know, old man, that we owls were once venerated in noble Athens? I was no less than the companion to Athena herself! But I was much more than a mere representation of my city, I was a symbol of the height of man's achievement, and I saw men touch upon all they could be, upon greatness itself."

The owl gave another heavy sigh in lament from the mournful shadows.

"Owl," said the old man. "Truly you are no augury. I delight in you, for you are a great figure, with eyes that terrify the gaze of man. I hold you in awe. And even if man is now haunted by imps of his own imagination, and even if the erudite can only think of coins required to cross the Styx, then at least they think of *your* coins, for the Athenians trusted you and stamped your image on their silver and knew that with you they had their full weight in measure."

"Old man, do you know why my call sounds a doleful note?"

"I can guess that for some reason you are sad."

"Yes old man, I am weeping for my lost children, for my great Athenians. They have misplaced their innocence, so I weep."

"Tell me, how did this happen?"

"My children were once natural and wild. They saw life all around them and felt their part in it. And they paid homage to life and nature and all that was reckless within. Dionysius led the way for them. They stood in awe of death, as in awe of life, and that gave birth to the tragedy. And they learnt the great secret that tragedy is nature and thus should only be approached with an embrace.

"So they performed tragic theatres, and the chorus was the people, and the people did not sense that they were merely watching a spectacle, but instead were transformed into a truly theurgic state, and walked with the Gods, and in doing so they accepted tragedy, and by that action also conquered tragedy."

"Truly, these men were great men." said the old man.

"Yes, yes!" said the owl with a heightened hoot.

"But what happened to your great men?" asked the old man.

"A dark prophet appeared, a great man of great thought, and without even realizing what he was doing he brought my children down from their heights on Olympus."

"What was his name?"

The owl hesitated, as if to harness all his reserves just to utter the name. He lowered his voice to a whisper.

"Socrates."

"Yes Socrates," replied the old man. "The best and the worst of men."

"Truly," said the owl, "does he represent the turning point in the history of your kin. He was the man who signaled your fall."

"Ah, yes," said the old man with a frown. "We are now a herd so docile that we don't even think of Socrates as our *bête noire*. We now take our calendar from Jesus Christ, as low as we have stooped."

The owl sighed deeply.

"How I watched this man as he conversed in his academy, as he sat up by lamplight late into the night, thinking deep thoughts with his passed-on progenitor. Oh, and the development of his logic, his ruinous logic, that has set the pattern of man's thought ever since."

"Except for the prolonged religious ages when we collectively deceived ourselves," added the old man.

"Oh, how low you have stooped mankind," bemoaned the owl. "And I saw Socrates lead my children away, and they began to worship logic, and mystery was banished. Theatre became a laughable joke of a thing and people sat still like fools and were content to watch actors. And deeply did I weep, for I had never seen a greater farce than that scene, the stifling of the natural and uninhibited, that being replaced by man-made constructs designed to produce order, the line to the Dionysian already cut, the break made. And to see this greatest of all my children's designs, theatre, misused and abused, only deserving of scorn and derision."

"Yes, the triumph of the Apollonian part of our nature," murmured the old man. "The triumph of order through logic."

"But even Socrates knew what he had done," continued the owl. "For right at the end he questioned himself and he asked,

"Could not even logic have limits? Could there still be room for mystery?

"But by then it was too late, for I had lost my children."

"Do not grieve so," consoled the old man. "You never lost me, for here I am!"

"Old man and dear friend, truly I tell you this. Soon you shall fly on high wings with me."

And with that, the owl sailed silently off into the night.

CHAPTER TWENTY-NINE

The Tenth Story

The winter-tide had already stirred high up in the north and was heading steadily south, gaining impetus as it advanced. The first high clouds were but an imperceptible mist, but with their presence the old man awoke, for his senses were aroused. The old man recognized the first hint of snow from afar.

The old man became increasingly restless as the day progressed, and low and dark clouds with dimpled underbellies appeared on the horizon, creeping overhead, the light withdrawing post-haste, like an army of cowards retreating before battle.

"Hail the winter time!" said the old man excitedly, his eyes shining and dancing.

"Old man, you have woken me from my sleep," murmured the wasp.

"Wasp! Now is not the time to sleep. For now it is *our* time. Now is the winter time.

"*Monumental. Epochal.*"

"Do I need to thank you old man?" reflected the wasp, wearily. "Why have you stirred me? To remind me that my mind is dull and my body no more than a frozen husk? For as sure as I sit on your shoulder I am also too cold to move. Don't you feel how this breeze carries ice? And behold, it grows in strength! My body is beyond aching, beyond numb."

"Dear wasp. I do not want you to miss your great moment. It is time for your coronation, for your triumphal march."

"Old man, you may be happy lost in your delusions but do not impose them on me. I have heard enough from you and enough of your pointless tales, none more so than your last sentimental attempt. Agh! To sting, to sting! If only my aged body could work!"

"Ah wasp, even at the end you still love your venom the most."

"Old man, do you mean to torture me with another of your stories? For my ears have already been numbed by your words, by the confounded meandering digressions, by the miasma of swirling thoughts that pour forth from your cracked and sorry mind. For your stories were truly duplicitous."

"Duplicitous? Absolutely! In the most pure sense, for there is duplicity in all of nature. Surely, dear wasp, do you mean to say that in all of the telling you could not detect the simplest thread? That it is impossible to speak of one part of life without speaking of all, for there is interconnectedness in all. And it is only when the *great all* is embraced that man can conquer the ills and fears that pin-prick his life. Only then can man do justice to life and rise up high on the wings of angels."

Then the wasp slowly spoke.

"Old man, you are unlike your own kin. Your perception of the cryptic in life is in conflict with that proclaimed by your own kind. For what of those you call 'scientists'? Do they not claim to hold the keys to infinity and the essence of life? Is it really a wonder that they would consider you anachronistic? That they scoff at you for your dreams of magic and mystery?"

"Indeed they do!" the old man laughed. "But scientists are at the vanguard of confronting the great mystery itself, and thus they still gain honour. Nonetheless they are flawed for they disregard from whence they came. For they themselves are the progeny of Socrates and push Socratic thought to the limit and demand,

'*To be beautiful everything must first be intelligible.*'

"But what of the unintelligible?" continued the old man. "What of the mystery and the magic and the forgotten and misunderstood? What of the Dionysian? For even Socrates was obliged to ask,

'Is that which is unintelligible to me necessarily unintelligent? Might there be a realm of wisdom from which the logician is excluded?'

"Indeed, the greatest insight came from Socrates himself,

'when he admitted to himself that he knew nothing.'

"Oh wisest of men!

"And these most fortunate of Socratic spawn, these scientists, have drawn us farther and farther away from ourselves, gifting us with a mythless existence in a life led according to concepts.

"For there is the problem, right there,

'the lie of Socratic optimism.'

"It is that optimism that gave Socrates reason to suspect that all truth lay in mathematics, and that mathematics itself should be considered a religion, yet a religion so perplexing that it should be hidden from the many, a religion so bewildering that it should be reserved for the few. But consider our own time, when scientists cry out, 'Philosophy is Dead! The laws of physics are constant throughout the cosmos!'

"And yet now we see that those very laws vary across the cosmos, and that mathematics is not a concrete religion after all, that there is still room for the unintelligible, for the magic and the mystery in life. For those who postulate infinite wormholes to infinite universes fail to see the infinite wormholes within themselves."

The wasp considered the old man's words.

"Your path to truth is a lonely one, old man, for if you spurn religion and science, there is no-one left to accompany you. Tell me, old man, do you stand alone in the greatest of sadness?"

"No!" said the old man, emphatically. "If I were drowning in the widest and deepest ocean of the saddest sadness, I would peer deep into the fathoms and still find love. For if sadness is part of life, as I myself am part of life, then sadness too must be embraced.

'*All that exists is just and unjust and equally justified in both.*'

The old man continued.

"And this includes the darkest, most-damnable and seemingly abhorrent. For all life is truth and her call is clear,

'*Be like me! The Primal Mother, eternally creative, eternally impelling into life, eternally drawing satisfaction from the ceaseless flux of phenomena!*'

"So how could sadness afflict me?" laughed the old man. "In such a life there is only triumph and delight. And with this triumph over tragedy, I am not merely a man or even a philosophical-artist, but have '*become a work of art*' and live not as an individual but *as '*the single living thing, merged with its creative delight.*'"

"And herein we face the great question, for *what* is man to live for? The will to survive? The will to power? Or even, perhaps, the will to create?"

"For creation is change and is intertwined with the evolution of all life."

The wasp huddled down, bracing itself against the cold.

"Little wasp," said the old man. "You are welcome on my shoulder, for this is our story. Use me to shield yourself against the cold, for as surely as I speak you are my brother."

"This story, this story," sighed the somnolent wasp. "What do you mean by all this?"

"Little wasp, now is the time for us to take our leave. The skies grow dark. Feel how the wind blows? A grey veil like a shield is on the horizon and moving this way. Our time here is nigh. Join me as my friend on this final journey."

"Old man, I feel old and weary now. Could it be that we may go together as friends instead of enemies?"

"Follow me," said the old man. "For I love you, and *this* is your story."

"But such talk scares me old man. How should I hold myself in the face of what is next?"

"Dear friend," said the old man. "Let us face forward together, confidently, with courage and valour and no feeble trembling, for all life travels the same path. Let us hold our heads up high and rejoice as we rejoiced upon being born, and bear ourselves honourably and with triumphant heart."

"Old man," said the wasp. "I am thankful that you are my friend. But grant me one last tale. Tell me something appropriate to this great moment. Tell me something to fortify me and act as a balm for my fears. Tell me a tale of the magic and mystery that is this life. Tell me a tale of the unity of all, including that to where we travel. Tell me something of the truth for which you searched and found."

"Dearest wasp, I will tell you something of the truth that I found. I searched for a lifetime only to discover that truth was right there at the beginning, in the childlike state, but was stolen from me by adulthood, hidden from me by adulthood, until I discovered it had been there all the time.

"For then I knew, that to live as a child is to have achieved '*mature manhood.*'"

"There is one last thing," said the wasp. "Something pinches at the back of my thoughts and calls to me as if from the realms of magic and mystery. And thus it speaks, 'What of the twelfth story, what of the twelfth test, for now I know that there should have been twelve?'"

"Dear wasp," said the old man. Let me explain this riddle for you. For yes, there are twelve, with one left unsaid. When men built cathedrals, in dark and gloomy times, there was but one feature in the edifice that did justice to God."

"And what was this feature, old man?"

"The builders left one stone unfinished, because they considered it impious to build something so beautiful that it could be compared to the creator.

"So it is with your tests, my stories. This moment is the tenth story, a living tale as we embark on our final journey. The eleventh story comes next, and is the balm to soothe you in your moment of passing. But the twelfth story belongs to the unknown and is of the beyond, of the realms of rebirth and regeneration. Therein the cycle will be complete. To know more than this would be truly Herculean."

"Ah," said the wasp, sleepily. "Truly old man, I am happy to be your friend as we undertake this journey."

"Take courage," said the old man, "for we take this road together!"

The old man and the wasp gazed ahead into the darkening yard, hypnotised and transfixed in reverie and rapture.

And then the first two snowflakes fell.

CHAPTER THIRTY

The Eleventh Story

In the valley, the days shortened and the farmers rested and only worked the winter crops. F slept under heavy blankets as the cold rains fell, softly strumming on the iron roof, and the wood crackled in the fireplace.

F woke early and sat by the fire. Then he headed down to the lagoon.

The lagoon was heavy with stagnant mud, a dark brown bed for thistles so thick that even the cows would not pass through, for rotting skeletons of dead trees, ghostly stripped skeletons in the cold morning shimmer, crashing down during high winds, and a haven for pythons and goannas and bower-birds, blue nests deep within the growth, all mysteries only to F, for no one else ever crawled into the bowels of that world, exploring, urged on by curiosity, that innate quality of youth.

Oh youngest and purest of boys.

F stood entranced where the murky depths gave birth to a vapor, forming a ghostly mist among the thistles and the mud and the rot, like a wraith passing through an ancestral cemetery.

The mist was of formidable substance, a heavy spirit rising from the deep, gliding upwards and outwards, signaling the arrival of the long nights and the low sun, whispering,

"Lay low and rest. Avoid the scythe and wait for renewal."

F crept down to this home of the djinn, drawn on by fear and wonder, treading deliberately through the fog, instinctively picking his way through the thistles and debris, crawling and ducking, immersed in the smell of mud and mildewed branches.

F wrestled with his fears, flinching at sudden movements but surging on nonetheless, an Odysseus drawn to a Siren, his thoughts in a trance, inebriated with the fumes from the crack in the rock and the judgment of the oracle, to where the spirits held council, the black silhouetted dead trees faintly outlined against the dim light, challenging him, daring him on.

And in the darkest depth of the lagoon, scratched and stung, cold and clammy in the density of mist, F stood still for a moment.

F discerned a breathing sound, at first bordering on the imperceptible, like the sound of an engine from far away, edging in and out of hearing. But then it was unmistakable and F's heart beat faster inside his chest and he froze in fear. And the breathing matched his own heart-beat and grew louder and louder.

But then, overwhelmed, he dashed, crazed, crashing back up through the scrub, as if chased by the hounds of hell, his heart up in his throat, up and up and out of the lagoon bed and into the rows of poplars. Up to where he could breathe again.

Oh land of wonders! A living, breathing wonderland of life! To dare himself to the gates of hell and emerge safely in his own kingdom, striding down the aisles of poplars, a royal guard flanking his path, to hear horns, as if it were his own coronation!

As he walked in triumph, the first rays of dappled sun filtered down through the branches and glinted off the small golden hairs on the back of his hands and forearms.

But suddenly the wind turned very cold. F stopped and looked up and saw a grey veil moving across the valley.

And then the first two snowflakes fell.